Freaky Fiction

20 Short Stories

by

Wayne Courter

Dedication

I especially want to thank my wife who spent many hours typing and proofreading my story. This is a special thank you for all of your support. Love that woman!

I also want to thank my daughter Whitney for supporting me, especially for encouraging me to keep on writing the next story and for telling me that they were all good stories. Thank you, Whitney, for designing the front and back covers and working with the publishers to set up everything necessary to produce a successful launch of a new book. Love that girl!

Table of Contents

Henry's Hindu Health Hut

"I've always enjoyed coming to Atlantic City to relax, drink, and gamble until the early morning hours."

"Me, too, Alfred, and it's good to get away from the kids for awhile."

"I didn't see that before. Did you, Alfred? The sign says Henry's Hindu Health Hut. The sign on the other side says that Henry invented the first whole body oxygen therapy capsule and that we can get a free consultation. Should we give it a try?"

"Okay, Marie, but I don't think both of us can afford to do this."

. . .

"Good evening, may I help you?"

"Yes, my name is Marie, and I want to find out more about your whole oxygen therapy."

"Come with me, and I will take you to Henry's office. He'll be with you in a few minutes. Your husband may remain in the waiting room."

. . .

"Hello, Marie. I am Henry, and I will explain the benefits of our whole body oxygen therapy. We are able to have your whole body absorb oxygen through its cells, not just the mouth and nose as in typical oxygen therapy. This allows your body to rejuvenate itself, and you will feel twenty years younger. We are getting close to closing time, so tell me, do you want to try our treatment?"

"Yes, Henry, I am going to go for it. Please have someone tell my husband so he won't worry about me."

"We'll take care of it, Marie. Now, the first step is for you to drink our own special blend of Columbian tea. This will take away your anxieties, stress, and any inhibitions that you might have. First, sign the application and drink your tea, and we will start the process. Then you can go to the dressing room and remove all of your clothing. When you return, I'll put you into our last capsule before we close for the night."

. . .

"Are you Henry? I'm Alfred. Where is my wife Marie?"

"Didn't they tell you she has already started her therapy treatment?"

"No one told me anything, Henry. I didn't know there were black Hindus, and what's up with the funny hat with the tassel hanging down?"

"The colors on the tassel denote the tribe we belong to in India."

"You sound more like you come from Indiana than India."

"I am second generation and was raised right here in Atlantic City."

"Excuse me, Alfred, but the whistle just went off, and that means that in two minutes someone will be exiting one of the capsules. Hello, Mr. and Mrs. Watkins. How was the experience?"

"I feel like I'm floating on air, Henry. It was really great, and I assure you, we will be back again."

"Great to hear that. The dressing room is straight ahead. That couple, Alfred, drove here from upstate New York, and they had a two for one coupon they found in a health magazine that I advertised in."

"Excuse me again, but there goes another whistle. Hello, Sarah. How was your experience?"

"I feel like I'm floating on air, Henry. It was great, but I definitely will bring my boyfriend with me next time."

"Looking forward to that, Sarah. The dressing room is straight ahead."

"Henry, those people were all naked! What's going on?"

10

"For heaven's sake, Alfred, how else would I be able to send oxygen pellets into the whole body unless it was not covered? Try to think this through or go back out into the waiting room."

"I see that there is only one capsule still in use, so that must be my wife's capsule."

"They will be coming out in about ten minutes."

"What do you mean *they*? Is there someone else in the capsule with my wife?"

"Yes, there is, Alfred. I explained to Marie that I had one extra person with no other capsule available, and Marie agreed to share her capsule if I charged her half price. Actually, she agreed to do so only if I gave her another cup of our special brand of Columbian tea."

"She better come out of that capsule a changed woman, Henry, that's all I have to say."

"She will, I can promise you that. You heard what the other patients had to say, right?"

"There's the whistle. Your wife will be coming out in two minutes."

. . .

"Alfred, what are you doing here? This is Adam, my companion in the capsule."

"I don't know how to tell you this, Marie, without upsetting you, but your hair is bright orange."

"I know, Alfred, and it's my fault. Don't blame Henry."

"Adam, didn't you see Marie's hair turning orange while you were in the capsule with her?"

"No, Alfred, it's pitch dark in there, and you have to literally feel your away around. We are heading for the dressing room now."

"Before you ask me why I designed it to be so dark in the capsule, let me just tell you that any heat from a lighting system would burn up the oxygen pellets, therefore, rendering them useless. Now, the reason why your wife's hair is bright orange is that she took a chance

11

and did not tell us she had a perm in the last thirty days. The pure oxygen pellets might turn the chemicals used in the perm to either blue, green, pink or bright orange. Your wife lied on the application and was also warned by me, verbally, prior to the treatment about the chemical reaction. She chose to take the chance. I really think this bright orange is the best of the colors."

"Are you some kind of nutcase, Henry? She looks like one of those freaks we saw on the boardwalk. The best I can hope for is to find a shop that is still open and buy a large hat to hide her hair until we get back to the hotel. Okay, Marie, say goodbye to Henry. Let's go."

"Thanks again, Henry. See you in a couple of months."

"Goodbye, Marie, and good luck with your hair problem."

. . .

Adam, you are the last one to leave. You looked very satisfied when you exited the capsule."

"You are a great reader of women, Henry. I have to give you that. Here is your $500. I will be back next Friday, and this time, I want you to pair me up with someone a little younger, and remember, she gets two cups of your special blend of Columbian tea and 45 minutes in the capsule instead of the normal 30."

"It's a deal. See you next Friday. There's nothing like a happy customer."

My Trip

I can feel myself starting to float upward, and as I look down on my bed, I realize that I am making a trip that I have never made before. I feel this new freedom and peace. Then I see the magnificent, bright lights, and I start to drift toward the middle of a brilliant light tunnel where I can feel the warmth of energy and love flowing all through me. I suddenly realize that I have now arrived in what must be paradise, where love and compassion abound.

As I look around, I see my older brother. "Hello!" I say. He replies, "The hell with hello! You took my patented idea and built a very large company and became a very rich man and gave me no credit at all. You could have named a building after me or at least placed my portrait and a plaque in the lobby of the main building. But no, you kept all the glory for yourself. I can't forgive you for that. Don't ever talk to me again, okay?"

Oh, here comes my ex-wife. "Hello, sweetheart!" "Don't try to be nice to me; it is way too late for that. I will never forgive you for leaving me home alone with two small children and no money to buy food while you flew off to South America. I was forced to write bad checks to the local grocery store in order to get food for our kids, and when the store found out the checks would bounce, they threatened to press charges against me and have me arrested. I had to call my father who flew in and made the checks good and convinced them to drop the charges against me. That is why when you finally did return, the divorce papers were waiting for you. I was so embarrassed that my father had to come and bail me out that our relationship was never the same. Worse than that, when you became a successful businessman and made a lot of money, you convinced our daughters to

13

live with you, and you were able to give them all of the material things that a single mother could not provide. You ruined my relationship with my daughters forever. I can never forgive you for that. Never speak to me again, okay?"

"Okay." Good, here comes my younger brother.

"Hello!"

"Let's get one thing straight right now. I am still pissed off at you for taking my new auto when you were home on leave from the Navy and ramming it into a telephone pole. I had to walk two miles to and from work for three weeks waiting on the repairs, which you never reimbursed me for, but much worse, I lost my girlfriend since I couldn't get to see her and take her anyplace. When I did get the car back, it was too late as she had already found someone else. I became very angry and made the decision to join the Air Force, which was the worst decision I ever made. I would end up doing time in the brig in France. I blame you for forcing me into that decision. Don't ever speak to me again!"

"Okay."

Oh, here comes my little sister. "Hello!"

"Don't hello me! I still can't get over the fact that you kept taking my husband to bars and nightclubs and turned him into an alcoholic. He died in his early 40's from cirrhosis of the liver and left me to raise two kids on my own. You were never anywhere to be found to help out and left the state never to be heard from again. I can't forgive you for your actions. Never speak to me again."

"Okay."

Here comes my brother-in-law. "Hello!"

"Welcome to Paradise! This is a great place as you will find out after you have been here for some time. I don't have much time to talk right now since I'm competing in a Wind Tournament, and I'm one of the

14

best wind surfers here. Also, I don't want your sister to catch me talking to you."

"That's fine because I'm not going to be staying here. What I need is to talk to someone I don't know and find out who I see about arranging my trip back."

"Hello, oh, it's you."

"Have we met before?"

"No, but I couldn't help but overhear your wife relating how you left her and your children without any food. I couldn't be friends with someone like that. Never speak to me again."

"That seems to be a very popular phrase around here. Maybe it means something other than what it sounds like. I need to talk to a female who might have a little more compassion for my situation."

"Hello!"

"Hello, did you just arrive here?"

"Why, yes. How did you know?"

"By the way you were wandering around and the dazed look you have. Did any of your family members meet you when you arrived?"

"No, I have no family members here as I am the first of my family to arrive here."

"Really? When I arrived here, I was met by my five ex-husbands who were so nice to me. Each one said he would not trade a single moment he spent with me for anything else. It was so nice and made me feel so welcome."

"You must have had a really special gift to make five men happy."

"Yes, I did."

"Have you ever seen anyone leave here and go back?"

"Yes, I have, but they were fighting to stay even though they had to return for some reason I didn't understand. Have you registered yet?

"No, I haven't."

"They will come to register you in the morning, and they will be the ones who have the power to send you back. Make sure to check with them."

"Great. That makes me feel much better."

. . .

"Good morning. We're here to register you and welcome you to Paradise. Do you have any questions for us?"

"Yes, I want to return, and I understand you can make that happen."

"We can, but in your case, it is much too late. Must be going now – many more to register. By the way, one of the things you will find great in Paradise is that you will have unlimited time to spend with your family members. Enjoy!"

Dean the Weather Machine

Monday

"Here at WWCA, your local radio station, we have breaking news tonight. We are adding a weather forecast with our 6 p.m. news report, which you have been asking for. I would like to introduce you to Willis Dean, also known as *Dean the Weather Machine*. He will be giving you your nightly forecast."

"I am very happy to be the one chosen to report the forecast, so here is tomorrow's:

It is going to be a really sunny day, warm with temperatures around 75 degrees. It would be a great time to take the kids to Hicksville where a carnival has just set up and is open for business. We all know how much kids love carnivals. Have a great day!"

Tuesday

"Dean, the phones have been ringing off the hook all day. All the parents who took your advice and drove their kids to Hicksville for the carnival ran into constant downpours that rained out the show. People are really mad and blame our forecast."

"Don't worry. I will explain what happened during the nightly forecast."

. . .

"Folks, I want to start out by stating that the reason for the change in weather today from sunny to rainy was due to an atmospheric aquatic cell that formed right over our area. This is when a low pressure cell absorbs all the moisture from the clouds around it, and when the moisture gets too heavy, it drops to the ground, which is what happened today. This is really a weather phenomenon that only happens about once in every 50 years."

"For tomorrow's forecast, we are still going to be in for more rain from this cell lasting most of the day. We thank the Good Lord for this pure and clean water for our fields and our wells.

If you must leave your home, be certain you have boots and rain gear on. If you can stay inside with the kids, be sure to let them know we are having a four-hour polka jamboree from 12 until 4."

Wednesday

"Dean, the phones were ringing off the hook again today. It turned out to be a sunny, warm day, but people were staying inside waiting for all of the rain you said would be coming. The kids could have gone outside and played. People are really mad at our station again. Let's get it right tonight."

. . .

"Good evening. I want to explain why the rain did not materialize as we had forecasted. A really strong northern wind ran into the gulf stream and drove the aquatic cell out of our area and to the west of our town. The sunshine was a blessing as it helped dry up the rain that had accumulated in the streets and on the highways, making it dangerous for drivers.

Tomorrow's forecast is for a cloudy, overcast day with the sunshine breaking through in the late afternoon. Have a great day!"

Thursday

"Dean, no phone calls today! Congratulations! Keep up the good work. Are you ready for tonight's forecast?"

"Absolutely."

. . .

"Good evening, folks. Your forecast for tomorrow looks like this – a beautiful day with plenty of sunshine, warm with temperatures around 75 degrees and a gentle wind blowing in from the South at 5 to 10 miles per hour. This would be a great day to take the kids to the new man-made beach that the town built at the lake. Pack a lunch and enjoy the fun in the sun and the lake water."

Friday

"Dean, we are having a real problem with the local community screaming at us today to remove you from doing the weather at this station.

What happened today was really too much. Around noon, the skies got very dark and winds in excess of 60 miles per hour were sweeping through our town. We turned on the police scanner and heard the police helping an old lady who had been holding on to a light pole and seemed to be okay, except that she lost her front four teeth, so they had to take her to the hospital for treatment.

We then called the police chief who told us that there had been roofs blown off some of our buildings and some of the barns. He said he received a 911 call from people at the lake who thought their wives and kids were drowning. A wind gust of hurricane proportions picked up a lot of lake water, and it landed on the kids and mothers who were on the beach having their lunch. They were able to get them all safely back to their cars and waited until the storm had passed to return home.

Dean, I have made the decision to suspend the nightly weather forecast until further notice."

"I am surprised that you allowed a little pushback from a few local residents to force you to make this decision."

"You have got to be kidding. All the damage that was done you consider a small pushback? We have already had phone calls stating people will pull down our tower if we don't remove you from the nightly forecast. I have been running this station for 25 years, and I am taking these people at their word.

The best I can do for you is to offer you a cleaning job until you can find another position in your field."

"I am not going to lower myself to taking a cleaning job when I am ALMOST a meteorologist. I admit I should have taken the NOAA weather map reading classes when they were offered, but I didn't think I needed them at the time."

"Dean, look outside and tell me what you see."

"There are demonstrators with signs that read *Weather Moron, Rain or Shine?* with a big question mark, *Dismantle the Weather Machine* and a large picture of a baboon with his finger in the air."

"I now have to go out there and tell them that we have discontinued the weather machine forecasts before something serious happens. If you want to go out and explain to them that you are *almost* a meteorologist and will be taking additional classes to become better at your forecasting in the future, and they agree to give you another chance, I might reconsider my decision."

"What did you say the cleaning position pays?"

"That's what I thought."

Dog Be Gone

"I hear the car pulling up, Harry. Let me look out the window. Oh, shit! You won't believe what our owners bought their daughter as a birthday present. A freakin' cat! Don't they know that cats and dogs don't get along at all?"

"This may work out okay, Jake. It just depends on the cat's disposition."

"Bull shit, Harry. My first instincts are always right, and I can tell by looking at that cat that there is going to be trouble ahead."

"Well, let's wait until we meet her and then make up our minds. They've placed her bowl right next to ours, so we will be seeing her tonight at feeding time."

. . .

"Nice to meet you. My name is Harry, and this is Jake."

"My name is Rosey, and I hope you two guys have no problem with my being added to the household."

"I have absolutely no problem and look forward to sharing the household and children with you."

"Thank you, Harry, that was very nice. How about you, Jake?"

"My first instinct is that we won't be getting along that well. We really didn't need a cat mucking up our relationships with the family."

"My instinct about you, Jake, is that you have some deep-rooted anger issues that you need to resolve."

"Jake is just going through a rough time right now, Rosey. His girlfriend Maggie who lived across the street just moved out of town, and he is still very upset."

21

"You seem to be a real sweetheart, Harry, and it is nice of you to look out for Jake. I have to leave now and spend time with The Girl in her room. See you both later."

"What the hell kind of cat says 'you are a sweetheart' to a dog? There is definitely something wrong with Rosey if you ask me, Harry!"

. . .

"Someone is at the door."

"Let's find out who. Stop your yapping, Harry. I can't hear.

. . .

"Hello. It says on this dog's collar that he belongs to you."

"Yes, that's our dog Jake."

"Well, let me tell you that Jake came out of nowhere and nailed my Ethel, and I didn't have time to stop it. You are going to be responsible for the vet bills if she gets pregnant."

"I apologize, and I assure you it will never happen again. I really don't know how he got out of the house. Thank you for bringing him back. Goodnight."

"We have to make certain that Jake doesn't get out of the house again, dear. Keep an eye on him at all times."

. . .

"Jake, I just heard you went out and nailed an ugly bitch. That must make you really proud of yourself."

"Listen, Rosey, you'd better stop being Nosey Rosey and mind your own business. Let's go, Harry, and play with the boys."

. . .

22

"Someone is at the door again."
"Oh-oh, where is Jake?"

. . .

"It says on his collar that this dog belongs to you."
"That is correct."
"I was walking my dog Sally, and out of nowhere, this dog runs up and nails Sally. It happened so fast that I didn't have time to stop it."
"I really must apologize and can assure you it will never happen again. Thank you for being so understanding."
"The only way Jake can be getting out of the house is when the boys come home. He must be sneaking out before they close the door. Look boys, you have to make certain Jake does not leave the house when you open the door."
"No problem, Dad. Consider it done."

. . .

"Well, Jake. I see you got yourself in more trouble."
"It's none of your business, Rosey."
"Well, I heard the owners talking, and if you do it again, they are going to take you to a vet, and when you return, you will be short some of your stud parts. I'm looking forward to hearing your high-pitched bark and watching you playing with a ball of soft yarn."
"You'd better leave before I nail you."
"How exactly would you navigate with two empty eye-sockets, Jake? Harry, how did you ever get lucky enough to wind up in the same house with Jake?"
"He isn't really that bad of a dog, Rosey."
"You are a sweetheart, Harry. I have to get back to The Girl and snuggle with her on the bed and watch TV. I'm getting hooked on those CSI reruns."

23

"Speaking of reruns . . ."

"Can you get the door, dear?"

"Hey, it says on his collar that this dog belongs to you."

"That is correct. That's our dog Jake."

"I was out walking my dog Ellie when, out of nowhere, your dog runs up and nails my little Ellie. I know from our neighbors that this is not the first time that this has happened in our neighborhood. If it happens again, we will contact animal control and have Jake locked up, and he will not be allowed back in our neighborhood. Is that understood?"

"Yes, sir, I fully understand what you are saying. Believe me, this will never happen again. Thank you for informing us."

"It happened again, dear, Jake nailed another of our neighbor's precious dogs. I have to take Jake down to the animal shelter and have them keep him for a few weeks until things cool off around here."

. . .

"It might cool off around here but not down at the shelter, right, Harry?"

"Jake, just try to keep your paws off the bitches while you're away."

. . .

"Good evening, sir. This is Jake, and I have what is probably an odd request, but I would like you to put Jake in a cage with a female dog, if that is possible, for a couple weeks. Here is a donation for his care."

"That is a very generous donation. I think that can be arranged."

"Jake was fine until his girlfriend Maggie left town, so I'm hoping a few weeks here might help him get over his anxiety."

24

"I see what you are trying to accomplish. Come back in two weeks, and we'll give you a status report on Jake."

. . .

"I'm here to check up on how Jake is reacting."

"Jake is not here at the moment. We had a young couple who came in and fell in love with both Jake and Daisy who was sharing his cage. They wanted to adopt them both. She wanted a female dog, and he wanted a male, so I told them they could take the dogs home. But, if you decide you want Jake, they will have to bring him back. I have to admit that Jake was very happy to be leaving with the new owners. So, what do you want to do about Jake?"

"Let's leave Jake with his new girlfriend. Thanks again for your services."

. . .

"Well, Harry, what do you think of the news that Jake won't be coming back? It seems they put a prostitute in his cage and then the two of them were adopted and went to a new home."

"I really won't miss Jake as much as you think, Rosey."

"I certainly won't miss him at all. I hope Jake doesn't come down with some type of disease. Know what I mean, Harry?"

"Yes, I do. You are a real piece of work, Rosey."

"Well, thank you, Harry. You are a sweetheart."

"Let's celebrate! Dog, Be Gone!"

Chicago Bound

"Harold, get the phone."

"Hello. Hi, Dad. How is everything going?"

"Just great, son. How is Chicago treating you and the kids?"

"No complaints. I was calling to see if you and Mom would want to come out to Chicago and visit with us since the kids are out of school. Now might be a good time for you to get to know them better because they are growing up so fast."

"Hold on, son. Maude, John wants to know if we could go out to visit him."

"Sure, why not? We could leave on Monday next week."

"We could leave on Monday of next week, John, if that would be a good time for you."

"Yes, that works. The kids will be excited. Did you get a dog? I hear barking in the background."

"Yes, your mother went down to the animal shelter and came back with Esther. The two seem very happy together. It is a swotzer, whatever the hell that is. I think it means it has some pit bull in it."

"I take it that you are not pleased with the dog."

"Let's not talk about it. See you in Chicago, son. Bye!"

"Do you know where the phonebook is, Maude?"

"What do you need the phonebook for?"

"I want to find a kennel for Esther while we are in Chicago."

"We have to take Esther with us. You know she doesn't eat dog food. She only eats what we eat. No kennel will provide that service."

"Okay, Maude, but her barking all the time is going to cause us many problems. You can bet on that."

The Trip Begins

Day 1

"Who is going to drive first, you or me?"

"You know I can't drive with my circulation problem. What if I have to apply the brake and can't lift my right foot off the floor? This is going to be too many hours in the car at one time for me to take the chance."

"So, I'll drive. Let's head out. Put Esther in the back seat."

"Pull over, Harold."

"Why? What's wrong?"

"Esther is car sick. We are going to have to let her ride up front with me."

"Okay, Harold, we can start again."

"We really should start looking for a hotel. It's almost dark."

"Stop, Harold. We just passed a Marriott Hotel. Turn around and go back. You will have to go inside because my legs are killing me."

"Okay, Maude."

. . .

"Good evening, sir."

"Would you have a room available for the night?"

"Yes, sir."

"Just two adults and one dog."

"I am sorry, sir, but we do not allow any animals in our hotel rooms. I would suggest that you try a motel which you will find on Route 16, two exits down."

"Are you sure no other hotel will take a dog?"

"Yes, sir."

"Okay, thank you."

"Did they have any rooms, Harold?"

"Yes, but they will not give you one if you have a dog. We are going to have to find a motel that will accept a dog in the room."

"Stop here, Harold. It doesn't look like a safe place to me, but it is getting late, and we still haven't had anything to eat. Esther is hungry."

. . .

"Welcome, sir."

"We are looking for a room for the night and have a dog. Is that a problem?"

"Well, we normally don't accept dogs."

"Would fifty dollars' cash make a difference?"

"Yes, I think we could make a special exception this time."

"Great. Is there any place to get food near here?"

"Yes, sir. There is Sid's Pizzeria about a mile down the road."

"Do they deliver?"

"Yes, sir. Here is their business card. Give them a call when you are ready. Drive around the back. Your room will be 103. If you need anything, just call the desk. There is a window air conditioner that you can turn on if it is too hot."

"Thank you."

"Maude, we have a room, but I had to pay extra for Esther. We will have to order pizza tonight."

"And a special order of meatballs for Esther. She loves meatballs."

"Order up, I'm hungry. They deliver, so have some money for the tip."

"Harold, this is probably the worst room I have ever been in. I am not going to sleep in that bed. I am sure there will be bedbugs in that mattress. I will sleep in the chair. I have to put my legs up because my feet are swollen from the long ride."

"Can you get Esther to stop barking?"

"She will stop once she has her meatballs."

"She better."

"What does that mean, Harold?"

Day 2

"Your turn to take a shower, Maude. Make it quick so we can be on our way."

"Open my suitcase, Harold, and give me a pair of my compression stockings."

"I can't find any in the suitcase."

"They have to be there. Let me look. Oh, no, how could I have forgotten them? We are going to have to stop at the pharmacy and buy more. I can't travel this distance in a car without my compression stockings. I will write down the exact description of what I buy so that you will not make any mistakes."

"First, I'm going to get something to eat at McDonald's, and then we can look for a pharmacy."

"The girl at McDonald's said there is a pharmacy half a mile down the road."

"There it is."

"I'll go in and get your stockings."

"Excuse me, sir, I am looking for a specific type of compression stockings. My wife wrote down what she needs on this paper."

"Well, we have a slight problem. The manufacturer has discontinued the large size in nude. We do have the same stockings in black. I am sure she would not want a medium instead, so that is all we have at this time."

"Okay, let me have two pairs of the black."

"How many pairs did you get, Harold?"

"Two of the black ones."

"You have got to be kidding!"

"They don't make what you want in a large size anymore."

"It is 100 degrees outside in the middle of July and you want me to walk around in a dress that goes to my knees and black, knee-high compression stockings? Do you know how that would look? People would think I just escaped from some mental institution."

"Look, Maude. We will be in Chicago in two days. We will find a replacement then, but for now, this will have to do. Don't you have any long pants you could wear?"

"Did I fail to mention that it is 100 degrees? Okay, Harold, I will have to get in the back seat, and you will have to help me get these on."

"How is this?"

"Ow, ow, ow!"

"Sorry, Maude, I'm trying to help not hurt you."

"Are you alright, dear? What is he trying to do to you?"

"I'm fine. He is just helping me put on my compression stockings."

"Okay, I was about to call 911, but if you are sure you're fine, I will be on my way."

"Nosey thing should just mind her own business."

"Don't be that way, Harold. Many a man has done bad things to women in the back seat of cars."

"Like what, Maude?"

"Look, just get the stockings started over my feet, and I will do the rest. I absolutely will not get out of this car until we reach Chicago."

. . .

"Well! This room is worse than the one we had last night."

"Order pizza again so Esther can get her meatballs."

"Okay, let's get an early start so that we will arrive at John's by tomorrow night. No more hotels!"

Day 3
"Hello, son!"

30

"Did you have an enjoyable trip, Dad?"

"Couldn't have been better."

"Oh, I see that you have the dog with you."

"Talk to your mother about that."

"Let me take your suitcases to your room."

"Kids, your grandparents are here."

"Hi, David and Katie! You surely have grown since the last time we saw you."

"We were just going out to order Chinese food. Would that be okay with you?"

"Sure, son, but order an extra plate for Esther since she loves Chinese food."

"Okay, Mom."

"By the way, Esther will be sleeping in our room."

"Dad, it's midnight, and nobody can get any sleep with the dog barking all the time. Can you take it to the basement? There is a TV and couch down there. I'm sorry, but it's the only thing I can think of."

"Don't worry, son. I bought some earplugs when I was at the pharmacy. With the door closed, you shouldn't hear a thing."

"Okay, Dad."

Day 4

"We are having fun with the kids, taking them out to eat for lunch and playing video games with them."

"Dad, you have been in the basement every night with the dog barking. Let me do it tonight."

"No, that's fine, son. I didn't realize there were so many great TV programs after midnight. Did you realize you have the Playboy channel?"

"No, I don't, Dad. That must be one of those free trial offers they give you for a week hoping that you will subscribe when it ends."

"I guess."

31

"Harold, I need your help. Hurry, we can't get Esther to wake up."

"Is she stiff?"

"No, but we have to get her to a vet right away. She must have had a stroke or something. John, find the nearest vet and drive me there with Esther. Harold can stay with the kids."

"Okay, Mom."

"I am sorry to rush in like this, but we can't get our dog to wake up. Can you have the veterinarian look at her right away? He said he will check the dog as an emergency visit."

"I am Dr. Leonard. We have checked out your dog and can find nothing unusual other than the fact that she is sleeping. The heart is normal, the breathing is normal, and the pupils seem to be normal. We can find nothing wrong. Has there been a change in the dog's routine in the last week or so?"

"Yes, Doctor. She has been in the car for three days as we drove from New Hampshire to Chicago."

"Did she sleep in the car for long periods?"

"She hardly ever slept, and she was also car sick."

"That would explain a lot. It seems she is totally exhausted from the long trip, the car sickness and the excitement of a new environment. I would like to suggest one thing, and that is to have your dog fly back home instead of putting her through another car trip – which would be a really cruel thing to do."

"We will do that, Dr. Leonard. Thanks for your quick response to our problem."

"You're welcome. Please give this to the receptionist on your way out."

"I'm glad everything worked out okay for you. That will be $350, please."

"How much?"

"Mom, just pay the woman and don't complain."

"That is the standard charge for any emergency visit. We will now have to cut our lunch from one hour to fifteen minutes in order to get our other patients back on schedule."

"Okay, here is my credit card. John, can we stop at McDonald's on the way so I can get five orders of pancakes for Harold and the kids for breakfast? Your father really doesn't like eating cereal."

"We really only need four meals because I have to go to work as soon as I drop you off."

"No, we need five because one is for Esther when she wakes up. She loves pancakes."

"Okay, Mom."

Day 5

"Here, kids, I brought some pancakes for breakfast. Esther is fine. She just needs more sleep, but she will probably be very hungry when she wakes up, so save some pancakes for her."

"Harold, I hear Esther barking. That is music to my ears. Susie, will you bring her out of the bedroom? Look at how well she behaves when Susie is holding her. That is because she can feel love and affection, Harold. She can also sense fear and rejection."

"Whatever, Maude."

. . .

"Kids, your father is home from work."

"Dad, could I talk to you alone for a minute?"

"Sure, son. What's on your mind?"

"Dad, what in the hell did you do with the dog?"

"What do you mean?"

"Dad, what the hell did you do to the dog?"

"Well, I was in the basement watching TV when it occurred to me that Esther's problem is that she suffers

33

from insomnia. So, what I do when I have that problem is to take some Benadrill, an anti-histamine tablet, and I sleep like a baby all night. I thought that would work for Esther, too, and it did."

"Dad, the dog only weighs 25 pounds. Didn't it dawn on you that the same tablet for a dog would be way too much?"

"You're a genius son. She slept for 24 hours after one tablet, so that means a half tablet would mean 12 hours, exactly what we need."

"Not really the point, Dad. Let's eat dinner."

Day 7

"We have been here a week, kids, and it's time for us to go back to New Hampshire. We're really going to miss you so much. Hopefully, we can come back next summer."

"Everything is packed in the car, John, so let's get started. I left $500 on the dresser in our room to use for the airline charge and to order food for Esther. She will be just fine. Thanks again for everything!"

"Well, Maude, this should be a great trip back since we can now stay in great hotels, eat in great dining rooms, sleep in great beds, and have a martini or two."

"You know, Harold, I was considering taking Esther back to the animal shelter when we get back home, but now that she is sleeping through the night, that is no longer a problem."

"Well, let's hope that airline flight doesn't revert her to barking all the time. If so, we will have to return her."

"Right, right."

"It was great that John was able to find your compression stockings online and have them sent overnight to Chicago. You really still have some great looking gams, Maude."

"Oh, Harold."

34

Four Lost Aliens

"SR, what happened? Are we lost again? This is the second time we have been lost with you as a pilot. We're in serious trouble this time. Did you fall asleep or what?"

"No, OR, I didn't. We went through a big radiation field, and it screwed up our navigational instruments."

"This is the reason we never get a newer spacecraft. You'd better wake up UR and MR."

"They are going to be upset."

"Where in the hell are we, SR?"

"Turn on the location meter and get the exact coordinates."

"Okay."

"Put it down in that field over there and hit the invisible meter so that no one will see the spacecraft."

"The location meter says that we are in Nevada."

"Never heard of it. Turn on the language meter."

"They speak English."

"Okay, put on the language helmets and turn them on to English, and let's see how we sound."

"This sounds really primitive to me."

"Do you think we should get out of the spacecraft and discover a new world? That could make our superiors very happy and reduce some of their anger since we missed our destination."

"Do you see all of those lights over there? Let's just space travel in our suits and land near there."

"Let's travel at high speed. It's too hot out here."

"Okay. Wow, those buildings are a lot taller than I thought."

"A lot of Nevadians walking around."

"We'd better land now. We seem to be causing a commotion."

"Hello, girls. You here for the Star Trek Convention? I really love your outfits. They look like they could have come from an alien planet. Good work."

"Thanks. Let's go in here where it says casino with all these beautiful lights."

"Hello, I'm your server. What free drinks would you girls like? We have a great champagne if you would like to try it."

"Okay, sure. What do we have to lose?"

"Wow, this tastes really great, and it makes me feel like having some fun, which we never have."

"Welcome to Reno. Are you girls here for the Star Trek Convention? It is just down the street in the convention center."

"Yes, we are."

"I'm going to the convention right now. Do you want to go with me?"

"Sure. Let's go."

"Look at all these people, and they all dress differently. I wonder if they can fly."

"I haven't seen anyone flying yet."

"Hello, girls. My name is Joseph Abound. And you are?"

"No, I am UR, and these are my sisters OR, SR, and MR."

"Oh, I see. You use initials for a name. You must be from the South. Would that be Georgia? Mississippi? Alabama?"

"We're from Alabama. At least, for now."

"Interesting, do you mean you won't be there later? You aren't illegal are you? Because that would mean you are illegal aliens, haha. At any rate, I can't get over this material and would have a great interest in buying it in bulk. It would be great for the suits I design and manufacture."

"We will talk to our grandmother and see if she is interested in giving you the formula for this material."

"Fantastic. Here is my business card. You can contact me or come by my office in Boston, Massachusetts."

"We will. Thank you."

"I think we should fly back to the spaceship and get a good night's sleep."

"I agree, but first I want to stop at the casino and get another drink of champagne."

"Hi, girls. Back again?"

"Yes, we would like another drink of the champagne that we had earlier."

"Okay, but it is customary that you tip your server, but I can see from your costumes that you have no pockets to carry anything. But, we can still give you the drinks as you seem to be very nice out of town girls."

"Oh, no. Look at the red lights on the transponder flashing like crazy. We are in trouble now. Who wants to contact our superiors at the base?"

"It is MR's turn."

"Let's get back to the spacecraft before they realize we're not on board."

"This is MR on spacecraft 491 checking in, sir."

"Where have you girls been? We have been trying to reach you for hours. You know the rule. One person must man the communication center at all times."

"We were outside cleaning the spacecraft. It had a lot of debris on it."

"We have checked our knowledge base and find that planet Earth people are basically of low intelligence. They have weapons that they use to kill each other. After that, they fill their bodies with mind altering drugs for no reason. This is not a society you want to associate with. We want you to stay in the spacecraft until all repairs are made. Keep someone in the communication center at all times."

"We understand the command, sir."

"Okay, who is going to stay onboard while the rest of us fly back to the convention?"

"OR has to go with us because she has been making a visual record of our visit."

"I will volunteer to stay."

"Thank you, MR."

"Back to the convention!"

"Hello, girls. I am Captain Kirk. Nice to meet you."

"Do you have a weapon?"

"Yes, I have my space gun."

"Do you use mind altering drugs?"

"Sure do, quite often in fact. I like to fly through space."

"You are the first Earthling I have found that can fly."

"It was nice meeting you, but we must be moving on now."

"It must be true about Earth people killing each other with their weapons."

. . .

"Let me have everyone's attention. The last thing we do when we are closing the convention is to choose the best costumes. The winners will receive $500. This year's winners are the three girls with the spacesuits standing in the back. Come up here, girls. Where are you from?"

"Alabama."

"And your names?"

"I'm UR and these are my sisters SR and OR."

"Oh, some visitors from NASCAR country, right?"

"Right."

"Here is your prize money. That is all for this year's convention, and we look forward to seeing you all next year."

"We'd better get back to the ship, but first we want to stop at the casino and give our friend a tip now that we have money."

. . .

"Hello, girls. Back again?"

"We have your tip. Here, take this. It's a $100 bill."

"That is really too much."

"No, take it. You were really nice to us."

"Okay, but now I'm going to get you two glasses of champagne to drink before you leave. Wait here."

"Here they are. You know, with the money you have left over, you can buy your own bottle of champagne at the liquor store down the street and take it with you."

"That is a great idea."

"Make sure it has a screw top."

"There's the liquor store."

"So, we have this much money left and want to buy champagne with a screw top."

"That will buy you nine bottles of a cheap champagne. Is that okay?"

"Great! Put it in three separate bags, please."

"Okay, ladies."

"Okay? No, it's not okay!"

"What's wrong?"

"I can't fly! In fact, I can't even walk straight, but I feel really great."

"I can't fly either."

"What are we going to do if we can't ever fly again?"

"Don't be stupid. We will fly again. Let's go back to the casino and see our friend."

. . .

"Oh, no girls. No more champagne. You look like you've had too much already. I think you girls are drunk the way you are walking and talking."

"We can't fly either!"

"Okay, follow me into the lounge and have a seat in the reclining chairs and relax. I am going to give you some black coffee and start to sober you up."

"You know we have to fly again."

"I know. Try to get some sleep. It will help."

"Are you feeling any better? Try to walk. It looks like you three are relatively sober now."

"Thank you again. We have to leave now."

"Let's see if we can fly."

"Yes, we're off to the spacecraft!"

. . .

"Where have you girls been all this time? The repairs, including the auto-pilot, have been completed for hours. I told our superiors you went out for a walk, and they are really angry."

"We lost our ability to fly for a short time."

"You didn't use a mind altering drug, did you?"

"Well, yes and no."

"I am betting on yes. Take off the language helmets, and let's get back to our normal language."

"You girls get back to sleep, and I will contact the superiors to tell them that we are ready for takeoff."

"Get ready, girls!"

"Who is in the pilot seat?"

"SR, sir."

"Oh, no! Have a smooth trip, girls. Call us if you get lost again."

3 Deadly Terrorists

"We are ready to put our plan into effect to set off three suicide bombs in Washington, DC. You have done a great job, John Brown, in teaching Abdul, Fiad, and Ramy English and making them familiar with the culture of the U.S. Since you have a U.S. passport, traveling back to the U.S. should not be a problem. We have your plane ticket leaving Istanbul, Turkey to Las Vegas, Nevada tomorrow. We will see to it that you are driven to the airport tonight."

"It is very important that you open a bank account in Las Vegas so that we can wire you the money that you will need to complete this mission. We also want you to rent a three-bedroom apartment for Ramy, Abdul, and Fiad. We have also already purchased their airline tickets, and they will be leaving a week apart. After arriving in Las Vegas, they will take a taxi to your residence and then you can take them to their apartment. At no time do we want you communicating with them by phone or email. There must be no written or recorded record between you and them. When you need to communicate with them, you will have to go to their apartment."

"We will have them cut their hair short, remove all facial hair, dress in Western clothing, and try to blend in as much as possible with other passengers returning to the U.S. They have each been given $1000. Their Syrian passport, although fake, fooled the airport personnel who sold us their tickets. So, there should not be a problem with their arrival in the U.S."

"You will be the only contact we have for this mission. The three men are committed to being martyrs and will be more than willing to complete this mission as suicide bombers."

"We also want you to video the chaos that will result when three explosions go off all at once. It should be a beautiful sight."

"Thank you, again, John Brown, for your support of our ISIS struggle. Good luck! Allah-Akbar!"

. . .

"Hello, John! Welcome back! I have kept your home exactly as you told me while you were gone. Your car is in the garage, but I did start it occasionally to keep the battery from running down."

"I want to thank you, Reggie. You're a great brother. You really thought of everything. Now, I need you to go to Best Buy and purchase a laptop and a prepaid cell phone."

"Sure, no problem."

"Here is $1000. That should be enough. While you are gone, I need to go to the bank and open an account. See you back here in a few hours. Thanks again, Reggie. I will be in touch if I need anything more. I am going to be extremely busy, so I will call you if I have any free time."

"To ISIS: We are all set up here. This is the account number. Need funds to rent apartment. Send ASAP."

. . .

"Now that Fiad has arrived, it is time to take all three of you to your new apartment which you will find very comfortable. It has three bedrooms and is completely furnished with a large TV in the living room and a small TV in each of the bedrooms. Remember, you are to have no cell phones or computers. We will only communicate in person. That means I will come by your apartment once a week to see if you need anything out of the ordinary. You will each be given $1500 a month for food, clothing, and personal needs. Take a cab to the grocery store when you need additional food. Your apartment has a large swimming pool, tennis courts, gym, and recreational area. Right now, I will take you to Walmart to buy the clothes you will need, including bathing suits. I will pay for your first purchases, but after this, you will have to use your $1500 for anything else you need."

. . .

"Here we are at your apartment building. You are on the fourth floor. Take the elevator to Apartment 416. Here you are, three sets of keys. I will return next Sunday. Should there be an emergency, and you need to get in touch with me, one of you should come to my home in a cab. That should not happen. It will take me some time to get the suicide vests made, so don't do anything stupid until it is time for our mission."

. . .

"Wow, this is really beautiful. John did a good job, and he gave us enough food to last for a week or more. It is too late today, but tomorrow I am going to use the swimming pool."

"We are, too, Fiad."

"Is this a great life or what, laying here at the pool and enjoying the sun?"

"Don't look now, but I see three girls coming down the stairs heading for the pool. Let's try introducing ourselves and see what happens."

"Okay, let's give it a try."

"Hello, girls. My name is Fiad, and this is Ramy and Abdul. We just moved into the building. I hope that you don't think we are being too forward."

"What are your names?"

"She's Maria. She's from Mexico. This is Juanita, she's from El Salvador, and I am Isabella, also from Mexico. Where are you guys from?"

"We are from Saudi Arabia. We are going to attend the University of Las Vegas taking courses in criminology."

"Did you bring some of that oil money with you? Just kidding!"

"Are you students?"

"No, we provide maid service for the Sands Hotel and Casino. We have the weekend off."

"Would there be any chance you could show us around Las Vegas, and then we could buy you a great dinner?"

"Not today, but if the other girls are willing, tomorrow would be fine."

"Okay, we will meet you in the lobby at 11:00am."

"When you call for a cab, make sure you tell them there are six people."

"Okay, girls, see you then."

"Juanita has a great body, but the other two could use, you know, the TV commercial Jenny Craig."

"It could be worse."

. . .

"Well, guys, as you can see, it is mostly the same thing – each street is filled with hotels and casinos. There are a lot of small businesses that sell jewelry, clothing, boots, hats, and there are a few museums. Have you been in a casino before?"

"No, we haven't. There aren't any in Saudi Arabia."

"Okay, let's go into the Wynn Casino. Most people like the slot machines. You can play blackjack which is what these people are playing. You need to get 21 or beat the dealer. At the crap tables, you throw the two dice and hope to get number 7 or 11."

"Did you want to try the slot machines, guys?"

"Go up to the cashier, and she will give you bills to place in the machine, and then you pull the handle and hope that you match three of the same."

"Okay, are you ready for dinner now? I'm starving."

"Sure, let's eat at a great restaurant."

. . .

"This is really nice."

"What can I get you folks to drink before dinner?"

"We will have three strawberry daiquiris."

"What do you boys want to drink?"

"Is the daiquiri an alcoholic drink?"

"Yes, it is."

"We never had a drink of alcohol."

"Do you like orange juice?"

"Yes."

"Okay, bring them three screwdrivers. A screwdriver is an orange juice drink."

"We are going to have steak dinners. They have great fish dinners, if you prefer."

. . .

"Here are your orders. Anything else I can get you?"

"Yes, can we have another orange juice?"

"Sure. Anything else for you girls?"

"No, thanks."

. . .

"Time to get a cab and go back to the apartment. We had a great time today with you girls, and we are feeling very good. Thank you, again."

"Before we leave, we wanted to know if you would join us Friday night in our apartment to watch movies."

"Sure. What is your apartment number?"

"436."

"Ah, we are on the same floor."

"What time?"

"8pm would be fine."

"We'll be there."

. . .

"Hello, girls! It's Friday night. Is our invitation still open?"

"Did you want us to bring our own screwdrivers?

"No, this is no alcohol night."

"No alcohol?"

"Come with me to the balcony. The girls are just starting to light up and smoke some weed. Care to join us?"

"This is marijuana, right?"

"Yes, it is."

"Okay, we will join you."

"Whoa! I am feeling good. This is some really great weed."

"Okay, let's watch some movies on Netflix."

"We have plenty of snacks. Weed will make you very hungry."

"Where are Juanita and Abdul?"

"They are in Juanita's bedroom. Would you two like to join us in our bedrooms?"

"Sure, thank you."

. . .

"Good morning. Anyone want to go into town and have a great breakfast?"

"Abdul, we are leaving to have breakfast. Are you and Juanita coming?"

"No, we will eat what is here."

"Okay, we will take a shower and meet you and Maria in the lobby."

. . .

46

"That really was a great breakfast. I love a glass of champagne to start my day."

"Do you guys want to come over again on Friday night?"

"Sure, we had a great time."

"We will need some of your oil money to buy more weed for the six of us."

"Here is $100. Is that enough?"

"That will cover it nicely. See you boys on Friday night."

. . .

"Do you realize that this is our sixth weed and sex Friday night?"

"Things are really going well for us, that's for sure."

"Abdul, get the door."

"Hello, John. We weren't expecting to see you today."

"Good news. The suicide vests will be here tomorrow, and we will be heading out the next day to finish our mission in Washington, DC. I will pick you up, and we will head out in two days. Are you ready for the mission?"

"Absolutely."

"We can't wait to become martyrs for Islam."

. . .

"We are about an hour outside of DC. So, we will stop and have you put on your suicide vests and coats and ball caps. I am going to park as close as possible so as to get a good video of the confusion and chaos for ISIS. Okay, you know where you are to go. Allah-Akbar."

. . .

"What the hell are you guys doing? Get in the back seat and bend over so no one sees you sitting there. What happened?"

"These vests did not work. They are defective. I was standing in the lobby of the Watergate Hotel pushing all the buttons and nothing happened. The same thing happened to Ramy and Abdul. You should get your money back and find a new maker of vests."

"I can't take them back."

"Okay, we have to get out of here now. Let's go."

"ISIS is really going to be disappointed as they already put it out on the internet to their followers to be watching today for a big event in DC. This is not going to look good on our part."

"John, pull over. We want to get out of these vests. How do we know that if you hit a bump or someone rams us, these defective vests won't explode?"

"No, we have to keep them as proof that they are defective."

"Okay, John. I am going to put my vest on the seat next to you, and I'm going to take the bus the rest of the way back to Vegas."

"Me, too, John."

"Okay, okay, get the suitcase out of the trunk and put the vests in it, and we will put it in a dumpster. I will be back in touch with you next Sunday with your allowance and bring you up to date on the purchase of new suicide vests. Keep reading the Koran and praying for success."

"That worked our really well. I figure we have at least six more weed and sex nights before John can get another set of vests."

. . .

"Hello, guys. Here is your allowance, and ISIS has contacted someone to make the new vests in Los Angeles. They said we should have them in four weeks.

I have to meet them halfway in Reno, Nevada. As soon as we have them, we will try this mission again."

"Anything I can do for you now?"

"Yes, John. Could you take us to Walmart to pick up personal things that we need before we go on the mission?"

"Okay, let's go. I could use some items also, so I'll go with you."

"I don't need anything, John, so leave the keys so I can listen to some music."

"Okay, Ramy, if you're sure. Start the car every ten minutes or so, so as not to run down the battery."

"Okay, John."

. . .

"Well, the good news is that we still have at least four weed and sex nights. Tomorrow, I am going into town to play the slot machines. I feel really lucky."

"You'd better leave some of your money here, Abdul, because last time you lost it all, and we had to pay for your cab fare when you got back."

"Okay."

"Hello, John. What is the latest?"

"I am going to Reno tomorrow to pick up the suicide vests, and we are all set to go back to DC in two days, so get everything lined up."

"Okay, let's hope we are successful this time."

"We'd better be or we will die one way or another."

. . .

"Let's stop at a motel for the night and get an early start tomorrow, which will put us in DC at 11:00am. That will mean the restaurants will be crowded by noon."

"This looks like a rather bad neighborhood, John."

"These are my brothers and sisters, and they can be trusted."

. . .

"We are just an hour from DC. We will stop at the next parking lot so you can put on your vests and coats and arrive in DC at exactly noon."

"Okay, I will get the vests out of the trunk, and you guys can put them on along with your coats."

"What the hell happened? The vests and suitcases are not in the trunk."

"Did you forget to bring them, John?"

"Hell, no. Someone at the motel broke into our trunk and took the suitcase. How will we ever explain this to ISIS?"

"Looks like not all your brothers and sisters could be trusted, John."

"Let's head back to Las Vegas. I need a good excuse as to how we failed this time."

"My father always taught us that the truth is the best policy when confronting a situation like this."

"Oh, thanks, Ramy, for all your ideas."

"Getting ready for a second suicide bombing and failing has affected me psychologically."

"Me, too. I am feeling very anxious and nervous. How about you, Abdul?"

"The only thing that disturbs me is missing the weed and sex night."

"What are you talking about, Abdul? Have you succumbed to the evil ways of the Great Satan?"

"Relax, John. Weed and sex night is a show we watch on the Home and Garden channel. It explores human behavior."

"Okay, Abdul. For a moment, I thought you might be involved in something else."

"John, we never leave the apartment building except to buy food, so how could we ever go against the teachings of the Koran?"

"Okay, guys, we are back at your apartment building. I don't know what is going to happen when I get home and read the emails from ISIS, but, I have decided to take your advice and tell them exactly what happened at the motel. I'll contact you later."

"We interrupt this TV programming to bring you a report on a gunman who was shot dead in the very famous Black Orchid Restaurant in downtown Las Vegas. It is reported that an off duty officer was able to shoot him before he was actually able to get his weapon into position to murder any people. We have seen the off duty cop getting into a police car, which we suspect would be to question him about what happened. That is all the information we have for now. We will break into your programming when we are able to verify the identity of the shooter. We do not know whether he was a terrorist or just a mentally deranged individual. Now, back to your regular programming still in progress."

"Can you imagine that? We have been to that restaurant with the girls. It is getting to be really dangerous to live in the U.S. You never know when someone is going to pull a semi-automatic and start shooting."

"Yeah, I know, Abdul."

"We are breaking into your regular programming because the would-be shooter has been identified as John Brown who was born and raised in Las Vegas. He is 29 years old, and we have verified that he was in Syria fighting with ISIS for one year and had just returned to the U.S. three months ago. He, apparently, was not under FBI surveillance since his return. The FBI is now taking his computer and cell phone from his house to see if they can find out if any other people were involved in the attack. That is all we have at this time. Now, back to your regular programming in progress."

"Why was John trying to do this on his own?"

"He wanted to prove to ISIS that he was loyal and that the failure to complete the mission was his fault. He really wanted to become a martyr and knew that he would be killed. It looks like we were partially responsible for pushing him over the edge. Our lying to him about the vests being defective didn't help, and then taking them out of the trunk and putting them in the dumpster at the motel didn't help either. We didn't think far enough ahead."

"Now what do we do? No money, and possibly the FBI will track us down."

"We will need a Plan B soon."

"Where are you going, Abdul?"

"To talk to Juanita. She has been through this type of immigrant ordeal herself, and I think she can give us good advice as to what to do next."

"Okay, give it a try, Abdul."

. . .

"Juanita suggests that we do the same thing that she did, and that is to go to the American Consulate in town and tell them that we want to apply as refugees and that if we go back to Syria, we will be killed either by Assad or ISIS. If they believe us, we have a good chance of being granted refugee status."

"Okay, let's head out now. We have to leave this apartment as soon as possible in case the FBI is on to us."

. . .

"Okay, here we are. Let's walk up to the guard at the gate."

"Sir, we are from Syria and want to apply for refugee status. Can you put us in contact with someone in the consulate office?"

"Stay right here, and I will find out if they will see you.

I will escort you to the office. Linda Hartman will be interviewing you."

"I understand that you want refugee status because you fear you will be executed if you return to Syria. Is that correct?"

"Yes, that is correct."

"Before we can start the process, we must have a background check run on you. If that comes back clean, we can proceed with the process. Here are the papers you need to take to the FBI. They will report their findings to me, and if you check back in two days, we should have the results."

. . .

"My name is Dan Jackson, and I will be responsible for running your FBI background check and will give your results to the consulate office. How long have you been in the U.S.?"

"Three months, sir."

"It is unusual to have persons seeking asylum that speak English so fluently. Where did you learn English?"

"All three of us were raised in a Christian orphanage, and we spoke mostly English growing up."

"Oh, how interesting. Okay, check back with the consulate in two days."

. . .

"Okay, gentlemen, your background checks found nothing to disqualify you. Here are your papers which include a green card and a social security number so that you are eligible to work anyplace in the U.S. I have been asked by Mr. Jackson of the FBI office to have you stop by and see him before you do anything else. It is nothing that you have to be afraid of. Good luck with your new life in the U.S."

53

. . .

"We have been told that Mr. Jackson wants to see us."

"Hold on a minute."

"Mr. Jackson, good to see you again."

"I wanted to ask all three of you if now that you have a green card and social security number, you would have an interest in working for the FBI. We are in dire need of Arabic language experts. With your excellent English skills, you would be a great fit to interpret emails, text messages, and phone calls from Arab speakers. The pay is $75,000 a year to start, plus all benefits. Would you have any interest in working for the U.S. government? If you need time to think it over, let me know."

"No, no, we are more than willing to help our new country against such a dangerous world that is trying to destroy the U.S."

"You will have to take a drug test, which you can do right now. It will only take 30 minutes for us to determine the outcome."

"Sure, let's do it now."

. . .

"We found traces of marijuana in each of your samples, but marijuana is no longer a disqualifier to work for the FBI. Stop back in two days, and we will have your employee contracts ready for you to sign to place you on the government payroll. See you in two days."

. . .

"Okay, gentlemen. All your papers are ready to be signed. Here are your copies, along with your plane

54

tickets with your flight leaving in three days. We have advised our office to pick you up at the airport."

"Where are we flying to, sir?"

"Oh, I thought you knew. You will be working out of our main office in Washington, DC. You'll love DC. It is one of the safest places to work and live. Congratulations!"

The Spacecraft Restaurant
Part I

"It was good of Coach to give us these three hours before our basketball tournament tonight."

"We have to be back at the hotel by 7 p.m. Let's get something to eat."

"Check this out. The Spaceship Restaurant, where it says, 'The Food Is Out of This World.'"

"Let's go in."

"Welcome, gentleman. Please use the elevator to the right and take it to the top floor which is our dining room. You will be taking the last three seats. When you are seated, we will take your order. Just pull down the feeding tube above your head and tell it what you would like to eat today. Order anything you want. When your order is ready, a red light will go on next to the feeding tube."

"We want large steaks with potatoes and collard greens."

"What about dessert?"

"We'll have banana splits."

"Okay, gentlemen, relax and enjoy the experience."

"Did you see the lobby? It was beautiful. This must be a new restaurant chain. It will be great competition for the Outback Steakhouse."

"Reggie, they even have computers that are creating the sensation that we are leaving Mobile and going into space. Really cool!"

"Keyshawn, didn't they say we were filling the last three seats? Where are all the other diners? Let's get up and look around."

"Jae, they are all on the other side of the dining room. Whoa! Something is wrong here. They are all comatose. Lift the arm and it falls like dead weight. This means that they all must have eaten from that damn feeding tube. Let's go back and get hold of the man in charge."

"Reggie, that sign says if you need to contact management, push the red button next to the feeding tube."

"What can we do for you, gentlemen?"

"We want to talk to the man in charge of the operation."

"That is me."

"Who is 'me'?"

"I am A.I. I will answer all your inquiries during this trip to our base colony."

"What the hell are you talking about, A.I?"

"You are going to be guests at our colony which is a long distance from here, gentlemen, so I would suggest you sit back and relax. It will make the trip much more enjoyable. Let me know when you get hungry."

"Let me tell you something, A.I. You made a big mistake picking Mobile, Alabama as we don't take kindly to foreigners coming here and kidnapping our fellow citizens and especially our young women. When we find your ass, you better be ready to get your ass handed to you."

"We do not have a translation for 'get your ass handed to you.' Please clarify."

"Let's just say that you should have landed in Vermont where they would have met you with buckets of Ben and Jerry's ice cream and given you their latest flavor of liberal nuts with chocolate chips."

"We have to find this MF and get this damn tin can turned around and back to Mobile."

"Let's spread out and each take a floor until we find this A.I."

"Reggie, how are we going to communicate with each other? It would be really easy for them to pick us off if we are split up."

"We have our cell phones, right? Ah, shit! I don't have any service. Damn it, Reggie, I should never have let you talk me into changing to Sprint for that plan where they cut your bill in half."

"Keyshawn, don't you have AT&T?"

"I sure do, but I left my cell back at the hotel."

"Shit! Okay, we will stick together and find this bastard."

"Keyshawn, do you have your knife with you?"

"I never leave home without it."

"Rae, push the red button, and let's get A.I back on the intercom."

"What can we help you with this time, gentlemen?"

"We have a really large, sharp knife, and we are going to start going through each floor, and when we find wires, we will cut them until there is no light or power for your engines, and then we can float back down to Mobile."

"If you think that would be a good strategy, Reggie, then go for it, but remember you will be floating back to Earth at about 2000 miles an hour."

"If that is all, gentlemen, I have work to do."

"That A.I is starting to get on my nerves. I am going to enjoy cutting his ass."

"A.I, you better notify your bosses that we are going to lay your ass out today."

"We do not have a translation for 'lay your ass out.' Please use better English when talking to me, Keyshawn."

"Your education seems to be lacking when it comes to the English language."

"Don't talk to me about education. In the two days we were in Mobile, we had a chance to see two episodes of Watters' World on the O'Reilly Factor. Are they your educated people?"

"There is a big difference between English and slang."

. . .

"Okay, guys, time to start our search for A.I. Back to the elevator. Let's start from the top floor and work our way down."

"Here we are at the fifth floor. Let's go in."

"Wow, this is really beautiful, all the bright lights and a dance floor."

"Whoa! These assholes must really like to party. A.I, is this your party room?"

"Yes, it is. We love music and dancing to its fantastic beat. Do any of you like to dance?"

"I love to dance. Let me show you some of my moves."

"Wow, Reggie, that was a really good performance."

"Reggie, what the hell are you doing acting like Michael Jackson for these clowns?"

"What type of music do you gentlemen enjoy?"

"I like hip-hop and especially Master P."

"What type of music do you like, A.I.?"

"My favorite is the Space Heavy Metal Band. We really get to rock at their concerts."

"Damn it, Reggie, we have to get moving. Let's go to the fourth floor. Open the door."

"Wow, this is really cool. This looks more like a library, so serene."

"Hey, look at this. CD's from Berlitz, English as a second language. I knew he learned white English."

"No signs of A.I. So, he has to be on the second or third floor for sure. Let's go to the third."

"Damn, this must be where they come to relax after a long flight to screw up people's lives. Look at all those pipes and bongs and those headsets with those goggles on them. They must be into virtual reality big time."

"What are the chances we try some of their stash? We're not in a really big hurry, Keyshawn."

"Damn it, Reggie, stop with the bullshit and keep a sharp look-out for A.I, Jae."

59

"Well, this is the last floor, so he has to be in here. There is a sign on the door which usually means stay the hell out, but since it is in funny looking letters from their space alphabet, who knows?"

"Reggie, you know that looks a lot like Egyptian writing I saw."

"Jae, where in hell would you see that?"

"I watch the U.S. El-Alamin TV station."

"How in the world would they be allowed to have a TV station?"

"Al Gora had a failing TV station, and a bunch of Arabs ponied up 500 million and bought it. They knew the administration would okay the transfer as they were all Muslims."

"Well, big Al took the money and divorced his wife, lost 40 lbs., and the last time anyone saw him, he was with an 18-year-old beauty queen."

"It still pays in America to have no conscience if you want to really make big bucks."

"Damn, Reggie, I didn't know you were a scholar or I woulda had you take my SAT."

"Keyshawn, stop the bullshit and open the door."

"Wow, shut the door quick. That is the power plant for this tin can, and it must be 1000 degrees in there."

"Well, let's admit it, A.I doesn't want to be found. Let's go back upstairs. I am really starting to get hungry."

"Keyshawn, push the red button for A.I."

"I was just about to contact you, gentlemen. We are very close to landing, so I want you to be strapped into your seats because sometimes the descent can be a little choppy. I have a request I would like to run by you boys. We would very much like to learn how to play basketball and would make your life very comfortable during your stay here so that you can do that. We have the most incredible look-alike Beyoncé women that you have ever seen. You can have them in exchange for teaching us how to play basketball."

"Sorry, we are all gay, so that bullshit won't work on us."

"We have no translation for 'gay.' What is that?"

"We are homosexuals."

"Okay, got it. We will have large, beautiful men waiting for you when you disembark."

"A.I, look, you need to understand when we are kidding."

"A sense of humor was not programmed into me. Sorry about that."

"Look, I am willing to teach you basketball – how to dribble, shoot three-pointers, and crash the boards. Just tell me that you will save two of those Beyoncé look-alikes for me."

"No problem, Keyshawn. They're all yours."

"Yes, Reggie?"

"I will teach you how to fast break, shoot foul shots, and rebound and, along with Keyshawn, we should have a lot of fun shooting hoops."

"We have no translation for 'hoops.'"

"Hoops is just a short name we use instead of the word basketball. An example is, 'Let's go shoot some hoops.' Now, I would also like a couple of those Beyoncé look-alike dolls."

"You got it, Reggie. They will meet you and Keyshawn when you disembark from the ship. What about you Jae?"

"You can hoop this! I am not leaving this piece of shit until I am told you will be returning us to earth and I will be on that trip."

"Okay, Jae. We do have another trip in about two months that will be landing in the Mexican jungle. We have a contract to pick up the relatives, employees, and friends of a guy named El Chapo Guzman. Have you ever been in the jungle before?"

"You can let me off in Mobile before you get to Mexico. It is right on your way."

"Okay, let me know in a couple of months if you still want to return."

"Where in the hell were you hiding on the spacecraft?"

"I was never on the spacecraft, Reggie. We handle expeditions from our base of operations in much the same way you do with those primitive drones that you keep losing in each other's backyards. I have to go now but will catch up with you guys later. Good luck!"

Spacecraft Restaurant: Return to Earth
Part II

"Men, I've called you three in today to make a decision as we are sending our spacecraft to Mexico in the morning, and I need to know who is going to return and who will stay with us."

"We've all decided to go back on the spacecraft to Mexico, if that's okay with you."

"It's fine with me as you have been really great guests, and we've learned so much from your visit."

"We have one request to make, and that is we would like to take our Beautiful Babes back with us."

"Are you sure you want to do that? Remember one thing, they are smarter than you are, and you could wind up becoming their slaves once they have absorbed all the information they need to fit in on Earth. Remember, they absorb information at a very fast pace. Do you still want to take all of the BB's with you?"

"Yes."

"Okay, be here tomorrow morning at 6 a.m. and come aboard. But, this time, you will be asleep for the whole trip, and we will wake you when we land in Mexico. Good luck on your return journey."

. . .

"Look at all those Mexicans lined up to get on board. It looks like they're going to abandon their vehicles, which means we will have our choice and be able to drive out of here. Let's get off this craft now."

"Amigos! Where you get those beautiful women? You find triplets who are gorgeous! Are there more where you come from?"

"You will have your choice of beautiful women, and the women will have their choice of great-looking men. Enjoy your trip!"

"Our choice of sexy men? Oh my, oh my! Juanita, Juanita, save me a seat!"

"Wait, Maria, did you see that? Juan grabbed the butt of one of those triplets, and he fell over dead! Let's get onboard now before something else happens."

"Jae, let's wait until they take off and then we will start to go through these vehicles and see if we can find any gas cans, maps, cell phones or money."

"Keyshawn, check this out. It's a beautiful van that has beds, a kitchen, carpeted floors, and a full gas tank. It also has a GPS that we should be able to use. Put the extra gas cans in the rear and tie them down. Put the cell phones up front with the money we found in the glove compartment."

"According to this map, we are closest to Guadalajara which is on the Texas border. If we can reach Guadalajara, we can get the American embassy to issue us passports so we can drive home. We still have our wallets with our driver's license, so we can prove who we are, but explaining how we arrived in Mexico will be a bit of a problem."

"We will have to say that we were kidnapped by drug dealers and finally let go when no one would pay any ransom. We'll turn off the BB's and lay them on the floor and cover them up."

"The GPS already has the address of the site where the spacecraft landed, so all we have to do is type in 121 Main St., Guadalajara, Mexico and follow their instructions, which will be in Spanish, so let's get the map directions. Who wants to drive?"

"I have the most experience. I had three accidents already and lived to tell about it. The stop signs and traffic lights are the same colors as in the U.S. So, I don't see any real problem. Off we go!"

"Reggie, lay down and get some sleep. You can drive when I get tired. We're not stopping until we get to Guadalajara."

"Everything is going fine, but I'm getting very hungry. Let me know when you see a McDonald's, Keyshawn, and we'll stop and get some burgers and fries."

"There is a McDonald's one mile up ahead. Let me get some money out of the glove compartment, and I will go in and get the food."

"I'll be right back, Jae."

"What the hell just happened, Keyshawn?"

"The damn McDonald's collapsed on itself!"

"Look at the heat coming from the ashes. All the metal in the building melted from the heat!"

"You were lucky you did not get all the way inside when this happened. Lucky the employees were able to run out of the building."

"Wow, that was close. Keep your eyes out for the next McDonald's. I'm starving."

"Another McDonald's is two miles ahead. Let's hope we have better luck at the next one."

"Okay, Keyshawn, bring back the food this time."

"Damn, the same thing is happening all over again. Another McDonald's destroyed! What the hell is going on, Keyshawn? Did you do that when you walked in?"

"It had to be me. What the hell am I going to do if I can't enter any buildings without destroying them?"

"Get in the van. We'll have to decide what we are going to do about this problem."

"Pull over and stop the van. I want to get out. I'm feeling very hot and need some fresh air."

"Reggie, wake up! We have a real problem here. Keyshawn is running down the road like a crazy person and seems to be infected with some weird disease!"

"Oh no, did you see that? Keyshawn's body just exploded, and the only thing left is the ashes on the road."

"We can't touch them for fear of getting the same disease. Let's get the hell out of here. Your turn to drive, Reggie."

"Jae, I don't know if we have this disease or not, so at the next McDonald's, one of us will have to go in for the food and find out if we are also affected. I'll go in first and hope for the best."

"Okay, but if I don't die from the disease, I am definitely going to die of starvation. Our gas is getting low. Stop at the Walmart and park at the end of the parking lot. I'll fill up the tank from the cans we have in the back of the van."

"Good move, Jae. There is a McDonald's at the end of the Walmart shopping center. I'm going in. Keep an eye on what's happening . . . alright, Jae, here are your hamburgers, fries, and a large drink. I'm not infected, thank God. After you finish eating, you are going to have to go in and get us some drinks to take with us, and let's hope you're not infected."

"Here are the drinks. I'm not infected. Let's head to Guadalajara and find the American embassy and get our passports so we can leave this god-forsaken country."

"Lucky we still have our ID's to prove who we are."

"We are still about 200 miles from Guadalajara. Wake me when we get there."

"Maybe I will wake one of the BB's and get some action. Need to feel the pulsating action."

"Reggie, are you crazy? We still have to think this all the way through. Where are we going to stay with the BB's since we don't have money? We can't take them to our parents' house. We don't have any jobs."

"Plus, I still want to play in the NBA. Remember that."

"Me, too. That's why we have to take our time thinking this through."

"Okay, the first thing we need to do is get rid of Keyshawn's BB. You heard what A.I. said, they are smarter than we are, and we won't be able to handle

66

three BB's with just the two of us. When we see another shopping mall, we will drop her off in one of their dumpsters."

"What are we going to tell the other BB's when they ask where she is?"

"We will simply say that Keyshawn and his BB have decided to stay in Mexico."

"What if they think we are lying?"

"We are not lying. They are both still in Mexico, right?"

"Okay, that's taken care of. Now, let's head for the embassy."

. . .

"Okay, here we are. Let's walk up to the gate and tell the guard what we are here for. Sir, we need to get back to the U.S. and get passports. Can you help us?"

"Follow me. I will escort you into the embassy."

"Many thanks."

"Good morning, here are our driver's licenses for identification. We need to get passports back into the U.S."

"How did you get into Mexico without any passports?"

"We were kidnapped and put in a truck by drug smugglers who were returning to Mexico. They thought they were going to be able to get a large ransom for us, but luckily, we were able to escape when the guard who was smoking weed fell asleep. Then, we made a run for it."

"I don't believe your story for one minute, but we will help you get your passports and get you on your way. Fill out the passport request form, and we will have to take pictures. Since the passport center is in Texas, we should have them back in a day or two. We will also give each of you $200 to be paid back to the government in one year."

"Understood."

"Since we have no way to contact you, we will leave word at the guard gate that you can pick up your passports. Keep checking with them."

. . .

"Yes, your passports are ready for pick up. Just sign for them, and you can be on your way. Good luck! Nice pimped our RV you have. I will give you one piece of advice. When you get to the border crossing and you have to show your passports, put a hundred dollars in each one or you will certainly be pulled over and checked for drugs with this RV."

"Okay, many thanks for the tip. Will do."

"Jae, checkpoint one mile ahead. Get ready. Put the money in the passports and pray we get through without being searched."

"Where are you amigos headed?"

"Houston."

"Everything looks in order here, so drive on through and have a good trip."

"Thank you very much. Have a great day."

"That was easy. Turn on the radio to an English station. Okay! Finally, some rap music."

"We are breaking into our normal broadcast with a very important announcement. The Mexican and American authorities are looking for two African-American terrorists who blew up two McDonald's in Mexico. They are in an RV with gold rims. The RV is bright blue with red stripes down the sides. The men are considered very dangerous, and under no circumstances should you try to apprehend them yourselves. Call the local FBI office or police department if you see this RV."

"Holy shit. They think we are terrorists. They'll shoot first and ask questions later. We have to ditch this RV now. Look in the glove compartment and see if the title is in there."

"Yes, here is the title."

"Okay, give it to me, and I will sign the owner's name and fill in the date and mileage. This RV is worth at least 60 thousand or maybe even more."

"We just passed a large used car and RV lot. Turn around and we will see if they are interested in buying our RV."

"Good morning, sir. We are looking to sell our RV and buy a regular car. Would you be interested?"

"It all depends on whether you have the right papers. I notice it has Mexican plates. Do you have the title?"

"Yes, we do. Here it is. How much do you think we could get for the RV?"

"The only deal I could make would be to give you this Chevrolet and ten thousand dollars' cash. How does that sound?"

"We don't want any Chevy auto. We want a foreign made auto."

"Okay, I have this 2010 Audi with only eighty-five thousand miles on it. This is a beautiful car, a teacher owned it and only drove it fifteen thousand miles a year. What do you boys think?"

"I like the car, but ten is not enough for the RV. You will have to come up with more cash."

"This is my final offer. Take it or drive out of here. Audi and twelve thousand cash."

"We'll take it as long as it has a current inspection sticker and temporary plates."

"You boys have a deal. Wait here and we'll get it all done for you."

"Jae, let's head for New Orleans. It will feel good to be back home. Now that we have some cash, we can relax a little more and make some better decisions."

"I'm going to use one of these cell phones to call my mom."

"Are you crazy? Too many things could go wrong. We will call moms when we are in New Orleans and have decided what to do with our BB's. We now have money and can get an apartment. We can't take the BB's to our mom's house. Just chill out until we can figure this thing out."

. . .

"I'm going to drop you off at your mom's house, and then I will go see my mom. I'll pick you up in the morning, and we will go see Coach to find out what we have to do to get into college for one year so we can try out for the NBA."

"Coach, this is Jae, and I'm with Reggie. We want to come by and see you today if at all possible."

"I have practice but will be free about 3 p.m. Where in hell have you boys been? We have looked all over for you. Your mothers have gone crazy. Have you seen them yet?"

"Yes, we spent the night at our homes. We will explain everything when we see you."

"Since we have to wait until this afternoon, let's go down to the park and shoot some hoops."

"Good idea, I brought a basketball with me."

"Let's see if you can still dunk."

"Wow, Jae! What happened? You jumped over the backboard! Are you okay? How in the hell are you able to jump that high? You have to try to dunk."

"See if you can also jump that high. Wow, nice jump and dunk!"

"We are going to have to practice just how much push off we need to be able to jump higher than anyone else and be able to catch the ball and slam it home."

"Wow, nobody will be able to touch us. We will be able to lob the ball to each other and score at will."

"Wait until the coach sees us doing this. He will faint."

"We have to come up with a reason that we can now jump so high when we couldn't before. I think we should say that we've been working out with magnetic weights

70

attached to our legs which stretched our leg muscles giving us the extra elasticity. That's the reason we were gone for so long. Let's just hope that the government will stop looking for the terrorists."

. . .

"Hello, Coach. Good to see you again. We need your advice on what we should do now in order to get into college to play basketball."

"The first thing you need to do is to pass your GED tests since you didn't graduate from high school. What makes you think you are good enough to get a scholarship to play college basketball?"

"We have been away working out with magnetic weights on our legs for all this time and want to show you the results. Reggie, head for the basket, and I will lob the ball to you."

"What the hell was that? He jumped higher than the basket and slammed it home! Can you do that all the time? Can Jae jump that high, too?"

"Lob me the ball, Reggie. How was that, Coach?"

"I have never seen anything like that in my entire life. You guys will revolutionize the way basketball is played. I am going to call Coach Atkins at Tulane, who never has a good basketball team, and find out if he has any scholarships left. Call me when you have your GED test results, and we will go from there. Your newfound ability is out of this world."

. . .

"Can I see Jae and Reggie at my desk, please? Were you two sitting next to each other during the GED?"

"Reggie was up front, and I was in the back."

"Why? What's the problem?"

"You both had a perfect score on your test, which hasn't happened in the ten years I have been giving these tests. Here are your certificates and a copy of your tests. Good luck, scholars!"

. . .

"Coach, this is Reggie and Jae. We've passed the GED. Any word from Coach Atkins?"

"After what I told him, he is holding two full scholarships for you and wants to work you out as soon as you are available."

"Call him back and tell him we are available any time he is."

"Coach Atkins will be ready to meet you at the Tulane gym this afternoon this afternoon at 3:00. Do you want me to go with you?"

"That would be great. We'll meet you at the gym."

. . .

"Coach Atkins, this is Jae and Reggie – I spoke with you about them yesterday. They have their GED tests with them if you decide you want them on your team."

"From what I hear, you guys are something special. Let's see what game you got. Holy shit! This is amazing. How in the hell can you two guys jump that high? Wow! Let's get the paperwork ready, and we will start working out in a few days. These are full scholarships which include housing and food. No money."

"It sounds good, Coach, but we have one request, and that is to have two off-campus adjoining apartments."

"That's no problem. We already have an apartment building where we house other student athletes. You will have to eat all your meals in the dining hall or buy your own food. Is that understood?"

"No problem there. When the paperwork is ready, call my mom's house. Thanks again for the opportunity to play for Tulane."

"Alright, Reggie. As soon as we get our apartments, we can turn on the BB's and start to enjoy life again. Drop me at my mom's house and call me when you get the word."

. . .

"What great apartments! Look at the large TV, computer, and cell phones. I feel like we're in a hotel room. You can lock the adjoining door from either side, which is a good thing. It's finally time to bring the BB's into our apartment."

"Okay, let's turn them on and start to enjoy their company once again."

"Hello, Beautiful Babes. You are now in New Orleans, Louisiana. I am sure you're going to find it a great place to live."

"Where is Keyshawn and our sister?"

"They decided to stay in Mexico. They felt that three couples were too much for them. They want to try to live a life by themselves. They said they would contact us if they changed their minds or had some problem and for you not to worry. Now, we are going to show you how to use the TV and computer. Using the remote for the TV is really simple. Turn on the power and select the stations you want to watch using the channel select button. The computer will let you use the Internet, and all you have to do is to tell it what you want to learn about and it will find whatever it is for you. You click on the website, and you will be able to read anything you want, but it will be a short version of the subject. Okay, are you all set with both of these?"

"Jae and I have been accepted at Tulane University and will be playing on their basketball team for one year. There will be nights when we are in other cities playing and will not be back to our apartments. It's late, so let's retire for the night."

"BB's, we'll be leaving for two days. So, enjoy your TV and Internet."

.   .   .

"Glad to see you back. We are not using the TV because no matter what channel we click on, it is at a 3 or 4-year-old intellectual level. So, we won't be using it again. As for the computer, we need more complete information on many subjects and want you to get us permission to use the library at Tulane. Can you do this for us?"

"I am quite sure that can be arranged. We will take care of it in the morning when we go in to practice."

"We need you to take us to a clothing store so that we don't have to wear the same outfit every day as we are doing now. Can you do this for us?"

"No problem. It will be great to see you dressed up, and we will start to take you out on the town."

.   .   .

"It has been three months, and we feel that we now have the necessary information we need to understand what happens on planet Earth. We have absorbed just about all the journals and books in the library. The last time we were there, all anyone was talking about was how the basketball team was 18 and 0, and everyone was very excited."

"Now for the really big decision we have made. About halfway through our flight back to Mexico, A.I. contacted us to say he changed his plans and decided to program us to be good will ambassadors to planet Earth when we thought we were ready. He also programmed you with advanced physical and intellectual capabilities. He knew how much you both wanted to play in the NBA, and he

74

had hoped that when your career was over that you, too, might tell your story to the people on planet Earth. If you did not, we would understand."

"Wow, this is the reason we can jump so high and complete reading a book in about fifteen minutes. We have a 4.0 GPA, and everyone is telling us how intelligent we are. Thank you, A.I."

"Now, for the rest of the decision. We have contacted Simon and Schuster, the book publisher, who gave us an advance of two million dollars to write our books and to go on a U.S. tour of all major cities. We must move to NYC and work for them."

"They will then translate our books into other languages, and we must travel to other parts of the world on a book tour. This will take years, so our relationship with you two will now come to an end. They will be sending a private plane in the morning to pick us up, since trying to get through a TSA search would prove to be rather embarrassing."

"We will be watching you play basketball on TV when your NBA team has drafted you. Since this is our last night together, let's spend the rest of the time enjoying ourselves. Lights out!"

Heading West

"Let's stick to the plan. You pull up out front of the bank at 1:55pm. The bank closes at 2:00pm, and there is no security guard, so I will have them lock the front door, pull the shade on the drive-up window, and have anyone inside get down on the floor."

"Give me my ski mask. I'm going in. Everyone down on the floor except you two girls. Lock the door and pull the shade. You girls start to put the cash in this duffle bag. Don't try to notify the police station or all of you will be killed. Give me the duffle bag. Is that all the cash you have? Okay, stay where you are, and no one will get hurt."

"Jump in the car!"

"Head out to the department store parking lot and park between two cars. We will take our chances of getting caught there, and if not, we will head out later tonight."

"You might want to take off your ski mask."

"Right. The duffle bag is completely full."

"How much do you think is in there?"

"I have no idea, but it's a lot of money."

"There go the sirens, and the police are charging down the highway looking for us. We just need to stay here until tonight and then head out."

"Let's take some cash and put it in the glove compartment and put the duffle bag in the trunk."

. . .

"Okay, it's dark and time to move out and head West. Goodbye, Illinois!"

"So far, so good. There is a hitchhiker up ahead. Let's pick him up. The police are looking for two guys in a car, so the extra person might help."

"Thanks, guys. It was getting cold out there. I really appreciate the ride. Where are you heading?"

"I am trying to get to Colorado to find a job working in a marijuana operation of some kind. Do you have experience in that area?"

"I had my own marijuana operation in Michigan before the cops busted it. I went out for something to eat, and when I came back down the street, there were all kinds of police cars and a swat team breaking down my door, so I just kept on driving. I am sure they have a warrant out for my arrest."

"What gave you away?"

"Stupidity. I thought if I paid the electricity and water bills online, no one would pick up the increase in charges, but apparently, when your electricity or water bill increases 40%, it's flagged and gives the police a reason to check out your address. That's when they found my operation. I had a complete basement set up with special lighting and was just starting to show a profit when they hit. I had an old car, so as to blend in, but it broke down, and I had to leave it on the side of the highway. I took off the license plate and threw it away. So, that's my story. How about you guys?"

"Let's just say that we removed money from our trust funds and also would not want to be stopped by the long arm of the law."

"We are Tim and Fred."

"I'm Allen. Glad to meet you guys."

"Likewise."

"Well, looks like we have another couple of people looking for a ride. Okay with you, Allen, if we pick them up?"

"Sure, the more, the merrier."

"Hello, get in the back seat. Where are you headed?"

"We really don't know."

"Let me introduce us. This is Allen and Tim, and I'm Fred."

"I'm Bill, and this is Linda. Linda graduated from high school this year, and her parents wanted her to go to college, but we wanted to move in together and take a year off first. But, they really put up a fight, so we decided to leave and start a life somewhere else. I'm sure her wealthy parents have private detectives looking for us, and as soon as we take jobs, they will track us down. Where are you guys headed?"

"Well, Allen wants to settle in Colorado. We didn't really have a destination either, so we might just settle there, too."

"I think it's time to get something to eat. What do you say?"

"We're starving."

"Let's hit Wendy's drive-through. Please buy the number on the menu so that it won't take as long to get our orders."

"Okay, let's pull over and eat and then we can proceed to Colorado. We should be there tomorrow morning."

"Does Colorado sound okay to you, Bill and Linda?"

"Okay with us."

"Tim, get on the Internet and see if you can find a rental house. We could set up a homestead."

"Here is a four bedroom, two bath house with a large barn on ten acres for only $1200 a month for the first year, but the catch is that we must make necessary repairs to the house. Sound like something you guys would be willing to do?"

"Hell, yes. Let's take a look at it."

"Mr. Evans, my name is Tim, and I am calling in regard to your rental property on the ten acres. Is it still available?"

"Yes, it is. You realize that part of the rental would be cleaning and painting all the rooms and making any small repairs that might be needed? I would, of course, take care of any large repairs."

"Sounds good to me. When can we see it? We will be in Colorado by 8:00 a.m. Could we meet you there?"

"Sure, see you then."

.   .   .

"Good morning, Mr. Evans. One question, is this property approved for commercial use?"

"Yes, sir, it is."

"Good, we are thinking about starting a business on the Internet and just wanted to be sure."

"Okay, let's go inside, people. I notice that your license plate is from Illinois."

"Yes, we sold our business and are looking to start over again in a better climate. What do you think, gang? Can we take on the challenge of fixing this house up?"

"No problem, Tim. With five of us, it shouldn't take long. Allen would like to take a look inside the barn if that's okay."

"Sure."

"Mr. Evans, we will pay you the first year's rental in advance in cash so that you won't have to worry about getting paid, but we would like an option on the second and third year. You fill in the amount you require."

"Sounds good to me, Tim. I'll have the attorney draw it up this afternoon. One other thing we would appreciate, would you have the electricity turned on and have the bill sent to us each month?"

"Sure, no problem. I will call you when the lease is ready."

"We will call you for your approval when we have finished fixing up the house."

"That would be great, Tim. See you at the signing of the lease."

. . .

"Tim, you won't believe this, but the barn has running water hooked up to it. It must have been used to water horses or whatever animals they had here."

"So, what's so great about that?"

"It means with some lighting and a few generators, we could start a marijuana farm and start to make some real cash."

"Let me think about that overnight and let you know in the morning. Right now, we need to find a motel for the night."

"What the hell is there to think about?"

. . .

"Hello, Tim. This is Sam Evans. The lease is ready. We have charged $2000 per month for the second year option and $2500 for the third year option. If this meets with your approval, I will meet you at the house to sign and give you the keys."

"Sounds good, Sam. See you there in about an hour.

"Thank you, and don't forget to turn on the electricity. Thanks again."

"Okay, gang, time to go to work. Since we need everything to set up living quarters, we need to split up the responsibility. Bill and Linda, make a list of all the personal items we will need. Start with shower curtains, soaps, shampoos, towels, toilet paper, and any other items you think we'll need. We will have Bill and Linda use one bathroom, and we three guys will use the other bathroom. Allen, make a list of all the cleaning items and paint, rollers, drop cloths, etc. The three of you will decide on which colors you want to paint each room. Fred and I are going to stop at an appliance store and order a refrigerator to deliver to us today, hopefully. We will also stop at Walmart and pick up five air mattresses with pumps that we will use for sleeping while we are cleaning and painting. We will have to eat our meals at McDonald's until we are able to set up the kitchen with all of the utensils we are going to need."

. . .

"Okay, guys. Take some cash and go to Walmart to buy what is on your lists. The refrigerator will be delivered tomorrow morning."

"Get something to eat while you're out. Bring back some burgers for Fred and me. We will set up the air mattresses while you are gone. The electricity is already turned on. Get some lamps also so that we will have lighting in each room."

"Now, we have one more decision to make. Allen wants to start a marijuana farm in the barn. We certainly could use the money this would generate. He would need help. Bill and Linda, would you be willing to work with Allen to set this up and keep it going?"

"Sure, Tim."

"We will give you a weekly small wage for your personal expenses."

"No problem, Tim, we will certainly be willing to do whatever is necessary."

"Okay, great. Allen and I will be going into Denver, which is only 20 miles from Leeds, tomorrow to buy a truck that we will need to get the items home from Home Depot and Lowe's. That way, we can set up the farm as well as purchase the plants to get started."

. . .

"How much does he want for that pickup truck, Allen?"

"$12,500."

"Is it really what you want?"

81

"Yes, it's perfect."

"Okay, offer him ten thousand in cash. Tell him that is all the money you have to buy a truck, and see what he says."

"Tim, we have a deal. He wants to see the money. I have already put ten thousand in an envelope. Give it to him, and make sure you get an inspection sticker and a temporary plate with the deal."

"Okay, ready to roll, Tim. See you back in Leeds."

. . .

"Sam Evans was here while you were gone, and he was really pleased with what we have accomplished. So, we are all set. The refrigerator also arrived, as you can see. We may need another one when we start to buy all our own food, but this will do for now. Fred and Allen are going to take the pickup and go into town to buy a used table and chairs. Bill and Linda are going to Walmart to buy dishes and whatever else we need for the kitchen."

. . .

"Now that all of that is done, it's time to get started on setting up the marijuana farm. Allen has found two used generators in Denver that he will pick up. After that, he will buy the lighting equipment from Lowe's, and once that is installed, we will pick up cement blocks and plywood sheets to place the plants on. The water must be a mist, so that will also have to be installed."

"Okay, Tim. I headed into Denver to buy the plants. I can only buy six from one dealer, so I am going to have to go to many dealers. I will need a cover for the pickup to hide the plants, so I will get that first."

"Okay, Allen. Have a great trip."

"By the way, I have some Canadian marijuana seeds being sent to me. These plants are four times more potent than the Mexican marijuana plants. It will take us about six months for them to grow into plants, but believe me, when these hit the market, we will have many requests for our product."

"Fred, looks like Bill, Linda, and Allen will be busy for quite some time, so let's take a breather and go into town and hit that country and western bar we saw."

"Sounds good. How much money do you think we have left?"

"I don't know, but the bag is still half full."

"Wow, this place is really packed. No room at the bar. There is only one guy sitting at that table. Let's join him."

"Do you mind if we sit here?"

"No, not at all. I'm Sam Jennings."

"I'm Tim, and this is Fred. Pleasure to meet you."

"You boys new to town?"

"Yes, sir. From your accent, I take it you're not from here."

"No, sir, I'm from Annison, Alabama. Only been here three months myself."

"What did you do back in Annison?"

"I had my own church and was doing really well until I was caught on video smoking marijuana, and I was all over the Internet. It was suggested that I might want to leave town and start over somewhere else, so I decided, hell, Colorado has legalized marijuana, so why not go there? How about you boys? What's your story?"

"We sold a software business in Illinois and wanted a change of climate, so we chose Colorado. We really like it here. Are you planning to start a church here? These people love someone from the South. They think all Southerners are really religious people and love the fire and brimstone gospel message."

"I don't have the money to start a church right now, but when I do, it will be very successful, I can assure you. I am now working at Lowe's and have to pass a drug test for the next ninety days, so no weed for me."

83

"Sorry to hear that, ha-ha."

"Since you boys just sold your business, would you have any interest in backing me in starting a church? There is good money to be made. I would be willing to take a cut of the collection for my part, say about a third, and leave the rest for you boys. Think about it."

"If we googled your name, would all the old social media reports still come up?"

"I'm afraid so."

"Well, the first thing we would have to do is hire a company that would scrub your social media items from the Internet. If you can do that, give us a call. Here is our cell phone number. I hope you are as good as you claim."

"Okay, guys, will do."

. . .

"Hello, Tim. This is Sam Jennings. Google me and you will find nothing bad. It's amazing how these guys cleaned everything up. If you were serious about backing me on starting a church, let's get started."

"You will still be working at Lowe's and then preaching on Sundays, is that right?"

"Oh, sure. It will take a little time to get the word out and build a congregation."

"Okay, let's meet tomorrow at your place to work out the details. Give us your address."

. . .

"Okay, Sam, let's get started. First, we need a name for the church. Do you have one?"

"Not really, Tim."

"What do you think of this name – New Frontier Christian Church?"

"I love it. It sounds great."

"Okay, let's find the building that we will be using. I think it should be halfway between Leeds and Denver so as to get both areas covered. How does that sound?"

"Awesome. Wow, I'm really impressed. You guys are incredible."

"We did some major checking on your church in Annison, and everyone said that you were a terrific preacher, so we are expecting great things from you. We'll give you one third of the collection, and we will pay all expenses out of our two thirds. Is this agreeable with you?"

"More than fair, Tim and Fred. God is really looking out for me. Sending you two guys is really a miracle."

"When we find the building, we will have you approve before we sign any lease or, hopefully, we'll just pay month to month. Either way, you will have to give the okay. We will be back in contact with you soon, Sam."

"What do you think, Fred?"

"Well, from what the people back in Annison say, this guy can really preach, and it will give us a good source of income, and with the money from the farm, we should be in great shape."

"Okay, let's get to work on it tomorrow."

"Okay, gang, we still need to get rid of the air mattresses and get beds and chests of drawers in each bedroom. I think Linda and Bill should go into town and check out the furniture stores and see if we can get each room furnished for $1000 each. If so, have everything delivered as soon as possible."

. . .

"Feels good to be sleeping in a bed. Good job, Bill and Linda. I think we are going to have to purchase a washer and dryer and each be assigned one day to use them. We will go back to the appliance store where we bought the refrigerator and have them delivered and

85

hooked up for us. That should be the last thing we need for the house. How is the farm coming along, Allen?"

"Just great, Tim. Bill and Linda are such a great help. It's a lot of work, but we are making great progress. What have you two guys been up to?"

"We're going to start a church."

"You're kidding. I didn't even know you were religious."

"We won't be doing the preaching, Allen. Get a grip."

. . .

"Sam, I think we've found the perfect building for the church. It was an auto supply distributor for thirty years that a couple who are now retired owned. They will accept a one-year lease with a thirty-day cancellation clause, which basically makes it month to month. It is spotless inside and has heat as well as air conditioning. They gave us the keys when we explained your situation, so let's go look at it right away."

"Good, we will pick you up in about thirty minutes."

"Wow, Fred, this is perfect. We can rent the chairs, and I have been telling guys at work about starting the church, and they will be willing to help me build the altar platform, and I'm sure that Lowe's will donate the building products that we will need."

"Tim and I will be there to pass the collection plate each Sunday as well as giving you your one-third share."

. . .

"Would you believe it has been one year since we arrived in Colorado, Fred?"

"We are really in great shape with the church doing so well. The congregation is still growing each week."

"Now that the Canadian marijuana is hitting the market, we are starting to see some really great profits from the farm, also."

"I think we are home free. The FBI doesn't have a clue who we are, I'm sure."

"Let's hope so."

"I think it's time for us to get on the Internet dating site and find some single women in Denver and start setting up Friday night dates."

"Good, but I have one rule that can't be broken."

"What is that?"

"They can't have any children."

"Sounds good to me. Let's get started."

. . .

"One of the problems we have, Fred, is that we still have only one car."

"Let's buy a car, a new one so we can impress our dates."

"Okay, what kind?"

"I saw a Lincoln advertised on TV that I would love to have."

"Let's go check it out. There is a Lincoln Mercury dealership in Leeds."

. . .

"Yes, sir. What can we do for you?"

"We would like to buy a used Lincoln."

"Yes, sir. We have six to choose from. Which one do you want?"

"The maroon one is beautiful. Let's work on that one."

"I'll have the paperwork done this afternoon, and the car will be ready to drive off the lot as soon as you deliver the cash."

"Great, we will return this afternoon to pick it up."

. . .

"Now that we have a car to impress the ladies, we can work on finding some dates on the Internet."

"Let's find a different date for every Friday night."

"I can't believe this will be the first date we have had in over a year."

"Look, I have a voicemail from Sam. He wants us to stop by his place tonight as he has something important to discuss with us. What in hell could that be? Everything is going great. Well, let's go find out."

"Hello, Sam, what's the important thing you wanted to discuss with us?"

"I hope you will try to understand what I am about to tell you. God has spoken to my heart, and I want to leave the church and start my own ministry. I would not be in competition with your church. My ministry would be to help homeless people with hot meals and give them a place to come when it is cold or they need some type of care. One of the Denver city council members who attends our service each Sunday said that he would see to it that grant money from the city would be given to my ministry once it was up and running."

"When were you planning on leaving?"

"As soon as you can find a replacement for me. I would like to give you one piece of advice and then I will move on. Try to get a pastor from the deep South as the congregation loves our accent and the way we preach the Scriptures."

"How would we go about doing that?"

"Put an ad in the newspapers in Alabama and Louisiana. I am sure you will have someone who wants to move on and start over."

"Okay, Sam. We want to wish you good luck with your new ministry. Don't tell the congregation until after your last sermon so you can introduce the new pastor, okay?"

"No problem. Thanks, guys. Without you, none of this could have happened. I still believe God sent you to me, and I thank him every day. See you on Sunday."

. . .

"Mr. Fred Fallon?"

"Yes, this is Fred."

"My name is Elizabeth Marie Walker. I'm an ordained minister from New Orleans. I'm calling in answer to the ad you placed in the newspaper for a pastor to replace the one that is moving on. The building we were using for our church services has been sold and will be demolished to make room for an affordable housing project, and rather than trying to start over here in New Orleans, I would really love to take over a congregation in Colorado. Do you have a choir at your church?"

"No, we never did have a choir."

"The reason I ask is because my mother is a choir director, and she can put together a choir that you will think is really angels singing from heaven. I also have always had a theme song played by local musicians, usually high school students, which is 'When the Saints Go Marching In.' The people just love the beat, and the kids get up and clap and dance. These two things really add to the services. Of course, my sermon is directly from the Scriptures and, with a little hell and brimstone thrown in, makes for a great service."

"I really love your accent and can imagine your sermons. Can you email me your background information and also when you would be able to come to Colorado if you are chosen?"

"Absolutely. I will do it right now. Thank you for considering me. Please call me if you need any information."

. . .

89

"Tim, what do you think of Pastor Walker's email?"

"I hadn't really considered a woman, but the more you think about it, the more sense it makes. A large part of Sam's congregation is women and children. So, I say call her and tell her we have selected her and set up her move."

"Pastor Walker, this is Fred Fallon, and we would like to offer you the position of pastor of the New Frontier Christian Church if you are still interested."

"God works in mysterious ways, Mr. Fallon, and I am sure he wants me to do this."

"The starting salary will be $60,000 a year, if that is agreeable with you."

"That seems more than fair."

"It will also include a home for you and your mother. We will give you the opportunity to choose the house where you would feel the most comfortable as well as safe. Leeds is a rural area, and we experience very little crime. We will also pay your moving expenses. Do you have an auto?"

"Yes, I do. Okay, give it to a transport company to send to Colorado. Call a moving company to pack up your belongings. Airline tickets will be waiting for you and your mother at the counter when you advise us of your departure date. Would it be possible for you to send a picture of yourself to my iPhone so we will know what you look like when we go to the airport to pick you and your mother up?"

"Sure, no problem."

"When you arrive, we will place you in a hotel for a few days. A real estate agent, Ann Harkin, will take you around to look at houses. Hopefully, you'll find one you like so that it will be available when the moving van arrives. Can you think of anything else that we need to do?"

"Absolutely not. This is more than I could have ever hoped for. We are going to make you very proud of the decision you made. We will call you back with the flight information and look forward to meeting you two guys in person. I still can't believe this is happening. Thank you very much for this opportunity."

"Hey, Allen. How is the farm coming along?"

"Great. You guys find your preacher yet?"

"Yes, we have found a pastor, not a preacher. Want to look at her picture on my iPhone?"

"Sure. Wow, this is one beautiful woman. Where is she from?"

"New Orleans."

"Half the men in Colorado will want to attend this church now."

"Does that include you?"

"I'll be there for the first sermon."

"Oh, nice looking set of wheels you got for me. It didn't really have to be a Lincoln."

"Don't go near that car. Stick with your pickup."

. . .

"How was your flight?"

"Perfect, Mr. Fallon."

"Please call me Fred, and this is my partner, Tim."

"Okay, please call me Elizabeth, and my mom is Mary Rose."

"Let's head off to the hotel and get you settled. You can charge whatever you need to your room. We will let you check in and, like I told you, a real estate agent will arrange the lease papers for us to sign, and we should be all set. Just give the moving company the address and the name of the car transport company, and we should be ready to show you the church and get you familiar with our area."

. . .

"Now that you are all moved in and have your auto, we want to show you the church and see what you think."

"This is a really great building. I love the altar and the lectern. How large of a congregation can attend each service?"

"The fire marshal says no more than 500, which is just about the number we had at last Sunday's service. When you feel ready to be introduced, let us know. Sam Jennings, our current pastor, is going to inform the congregation that this will be his last sermon and will then introduce you as his replacement. At that point, you should explain what you are going to add, such as a choir, and introduce your mother and also your theme song that will be played each Sunday. I think it would be a great idea, after the service, to shake hands with each person as they leave the church and see what type of feedback you get. After that, we will go back to the office and make out the deposit slip for the collection. I am sure you are going to be warmly received."

. . .

"Fred, I'm ready for next Sunday, if you are.

"I will let Sam know that it will be his last sermon next week. I also went by Leeds High School and met with the music director who is more than happy to provide his students to play our songs on Sunday. I told him we would be making donations to the music program, and he seemed really pleased."

"Great."

. . .

"Well, here we are, Sam, at the last sermon you will be giving here at New Frontier Christian Church."

"I have a special message I would like to convey to all of you this morning. This was my last sermon. I have decided to start my own ministry in Denver, which will be dedicated to helping the poor and homeless with hot meals and a place to find comfort. I have enjoyed my time here, and you have been a great congregation. I would like to take this opportunity to introduce our new pastor, Elizabeth Marie Walker who comes to us from New Orleans. Her sermons will be much like mine, taken directly from Scripture. I know you will give her a warm reception. I give you Pastor Walker."

"Thank you, Pastor Jennings, and we wish you great success on your new assignment from God."

. . .

"Elizabeth, it has only been four months, and we already have a problem. We have an overflow crowd because there's no room left in the church. I am going to have to tell them they can't come in."

"No, no, Tim. Tell them that there will be another service as soon as this one is finished. We are going to have two services each Sunday if we can keep this big of a congregation. They really love the choir and the live music."

"You have done a great job."

. . .

"How do you feel after conducting two services?"

"Great. Change the sign outside to say that there are now two services every Sunday."

"We are going to raise your salary from 60 thousand to 100 thousand for all of the extra work you will be putting in."

. . .

"Allen, where have you been going all these nights for the last three months? We notice that you're not returning until the morning. Who is she?"

"Her name is Liz."

"Anything serious happening?"

"When do we get to meet her?"

"If we decide to go to the next level, we will all get together for dinner sometime."

"Okay, Allen, good luck with your romance."

"Tim, can I use the car to go into Denver? I want to buy Linda a birthday present."

"Sure, Bill. Do you want us to pick up a cake and have a little celebration when you get back?"

"That would be great. Try to make it a surprise."

"We can do that."

. . .

"Hello, this is Detective Tom Collier with the Denver Police Department. Your telephone number was listed on a jewelry sales slip we found in Bill Watson's pocket. What is your name and how are you related to Bill? I am asking because Bill was murdered today in an apparent robbery. We will need someone to identify the body and also come to police headquarters to answer some questions regarding Bill. What is your name?"

"Fred Fallon."

"Are you related to Bill?"

"I am as close as anyone to Bill. He has no known relatives as he was raised in the foster care system in Illinois and never knew who his parents were."

"Okay, then, can we expect you soon?"

"First, I have to tell his girlfriend, and that will not be easy."

"I understand, but time is of the essence. Please come in as soon as possible."

"Elizabeth, I'm so glad I was able to get hold of you. I need a big favor. Bill and Linda live here with us and

94

work for us also. Bill was murdered today in Denver, and I have to tell Linda, but I need your help because she will be really distraught. Can I bring her over to your house and tell her while you are there so you can comfort her?"

"Sure, Fred. Mom and I will keep her here as long as necessary to help her cope with this tragedy."

"Okay, we will be there shortly."

. . .

"My name is Fred Wheeler. I was told to ask for Detective Tom Collier."

"Hold on one minute, sir. I'll tell Tom you're here."

"Hello, Fred. Sorry we have to meet under these circumstances, but we need to get as much information as possible. Our theory is that Bill purchased an engagement ring and paid $5000 cash. He then went into a bar, which we have confirmed, and apparently was showing off the ring to other people in the bar. We believe more than one person followed him out, and during the robbery attempt, he put up a fight and was shot. They left him in an alley. The problem is that we have no witnesses, no fingerprints, no shell casings, and no DNA. His wallet and car keys are missing. We need the description of the car and license plate number. Our hope is that we will catch them driving the vehicle or, if they abandon it, we would be able to get some fingerprints. This is the only chance we have of solving this case unless someone comes forward who witnessed the crime, but I wouldn't count on that. It was most likely a couple of drug addicts who saw a chance to make some quick money. We will canvas all the pawnshops in the area and see if the ring shows up. The law in Denver is that an ID must be shown when pawning something. We could get lucky if that happens. If you want to contact your insurance company and tell them your car was stolen, have them call me, and I will verify that we have an all-points bulletin out for it, and it was definitely stolen."

"I will accompany you to identify the body and also recommend a funeral home that we use when something like this happens. We will keep in touch if we get any breaks in Bill's murder. Thanks for coming in so quickly."

. . .

"Elizabeth, I just left the police headquarters and also made burial arrangements to have Bill cremated. How is Linda doing?"

"She's taking it really hard, Fred. We'll have to keep her here for several days at least. We'll do everything possible for her, but I don't want you or Tim to stop by just yet. I will call you when I think it's the right time."

"Thanks, Elizabeth. I don't know what we would have done without you and your mother. I'll wait to hear from you. Thanks again."

"Tim, I know you have been helping Allen all day to make up for Linda and Bill not being here, but we need you to go to the attorney appointment that we have scheduled for tomorrow. I will help Allen tomorrow. I'm still waiting for Elizabeth to call me regarding Linda."

"Fred, I just left the attorney's office, and he claims that our application to grow marijuana legally will be approved. I gave him 25 thousand in cash, and if it is approved, his fee will be another 10 thousand. He is also filing a corporation for us as the permit must be issued to a business. The name of Bill's Farm cleared, so that will be our new company for growing and selling marijuana legally. Keep your fingers crossed, but he seems awfully confident. This isn't his first application, as he pointed out to me."

"How is Linda doing?"

"I don't know. I haven't heard from Elizabeth yet, but I am sure she will have her in as good a frame of mind as is possible. See you when I get back. I don't think we should say anything to Allen about the application until it is actually approved."

"I agree. I hate working with Allen."

"Me, too."

. . .

"Fred, this is Elizabeth. Linda is ready to face the world again. She is not totally ready, but things are much better. She called her parents who were so happy to hear from her and want her to come back home. They really love her and will support her all the way without any blame for running away. I need you to pick up a set of luggage, and she wants to go back to the house and pack up her belongings. I told her you would get her an airplane ticket online and have it ready when you pick her up, which can be anytime you're ready."

"We will get the luggage and then pick her up today."

"Also, Fred, do not mention to her about Bill buying an engagement ring for her. We only told her that he was the victim of a robbery attempt. Please just leave it at that if the subject comes up."

"Okay, Elizabeth. I understand.

. . .

"Hi, Linda. Ready to go back to the house for your personal belongings? We have a set of luggage for you. Tim has purchased a ticket, and you will be leaving this afternoon to reunite with your parents. We are placing $10,000 in your smallest suitcase. This is the money that you and Bill certainly deserve for all the work you put in on the farm. As soon as you are packed, we will head to the airport."

"We want to wish you all the best under these circumstances and hope you will enroll in college and get a good education. Please remember, if you ever need anything, and I mean anything, you have our phone number and address. Please do not hesitate to call us. Send us an email every once in a while. Your flight is now checking passengers in. Have a great flight."

. . .

"Fred, I just got off the phone with our attorney, and we were approved for our permit to produce marijuana legally. How about that, old friend?"

"Incredible how things have turned out. Allen just pulled in. Let's tell him now."

"Allen, we have some great news. Sit down. You are now working for Bill's Farm, Inc. We are legal to grow and sell marijuana in the state of Colorado."

"This is fantastic news, guys. You really don't know how good this is. I told you that I would introduce you to Liz when the time was right, and that time is now. I may surprise you, but you already know Liz. She is better known as Elizabeth Marie Walker."

"You have to be kidding, Allen. You and Elizabeth?"

"Yeah, our plans are to go to Las Vegas and get married, and now we can do it right away since we are legal. She wasn't going to do it as long as I was involved with an illegal operation. I think it was great of you guys to name it after Bill. I really do. We are really going to make a lot of money, especially with the Canadian plants. We will be getting top dollar and won't be able to fill all the orders."

"What about the arrest warrant issued for you in Michigan?"

"Liz contacted a lawyer there, and he is getting me a plea bargain, so I will have to pay a small fine and serve one year's probation."

"Now we can hire people to help you. I never want to work for you again."

"Me, either. Wait until we see Elizabeth about hiding this from us all this time."

"Well, Tim, it looks like everything has worked out for us. I have used the trust withdrawal to help a lot of people."

"Let's get back on the Internet dating site and get some action for Friday night."

"Sounds good to me."

Roscoe and Jarvis

"It looks like the linen truck will be coming late today. We can finally put our escape plan into action. The guards will think we went on to chow. I'm climbing into the linen bin, and you'll cover me up. We'll pile linen on top of the table, and you'll put the bin next to the table. Stand in the bin, and pull the linen on top of yourself, just the way we practiced. There are eight bins to be loaded on the truck. Some are heavier than others, so I don't think the driver will get suspicious. Get ready to exit this prison and, hopefully, we will make a great escape. I told you that we have to keep it simple. Great escapes are always the ones right under the guards' noses."

. . .

"Jarvis, I think we can get out of the bins now. I don't hear any noise, and the building is dark."

"Okay, Roscoe, so far so good. Check this out, a bin of uniforms from Jiffy Lube that we can change into."

"Put that shirt back, Roscoe."

"Why?"

"The name on the shirt is Omar. You don't look like an Omar to me. They have long black hair, a full beard, and evil eyes. There's one with the name Sam. It will fit you even though you are overweight. Put the prison clothes in the trash can, and let's start to figure out how to get out of here."

"I'm curious as to why you were sent to prison, Jarvis."

"I stole a car and was on my way to Atlantic City to go to a casino when I blew a tire on the Jersey Turnpike. A state trooper pulled up behind me and ran my plate, and

I got 15 years just for stealing an auto. Because it was my third time."

"Oh."

"What are you in for, Roscoe?"

"Murder, 25 to life. I was working construction, and everyday this guy was bitching and complaining about something, and I just got tired of him. He fell off the 19th floor to his death."

"Why did they blame you?"

"There was a film crew making a video for showing the bank the progress we were making, and there I was, with a starring role."

"Let's figure out how to get the hell out of here. The front and back doors and all of the windows are wired to an alarm system. I expected the cops to be showing up by now. They know we had to have escaped using the laundry truck. They are really short on guards, and they have been missing bed checks the last month or so. Hopefully, that is what's happening tonight."

"Check out the office. Do you see what I see? A window air conditioning unit. Break down the door, and let's remove the air unit and escape through the opening. Grab those steel bars and start to remove the AC unit."

"This is going to be easy. It's sitting right on a platform, so we can remove it by just pulling it straight out of the wall."

"This opening is large enough for you to reach the outside. I am too big, so we will have to make the hole bigger."

"This wall is made of cement blocks. How in the hell are we going to break them?"

"I have a plan, Roscoe. First, I have to reach the outside. I'm going to drop down to the ground."

"Jarvis, why are you going out head first? Wouldn't it be better to go out feet first? Here, let me help you up."

"I'm going to hotwire one of the trucks and back it into the wall until we have an opening big enough for you. Stay back."

"That was a good try, but you will have to do it again to break it completely."

"Alright, Jarvis. Before you come out, check the desk and see if there are any valuables or cash. Use the iron bar to bust open the desk."

"Guess what we have here? A cashbox with quite a bit of money."

"Should I take the cash out?"

"No, just hand me the box and get into the truck. We have plenty of gas, so let's head down the road, Roscoe, because pretty soon our black asses will be all over TV and the Internet."

"Let me know when you see a shopping mall. Now that we have some money, we can buy clothing and get rid of these Jiffy Lube uniforms."

"Pull over, there's a Kmart where we can park the truck and get our clothing. Empty the cashbox, and let's buy our clothes and change in the Kmart men's room. I think we should buy sneakers, jeans, hats, and a hoodie."

"Okay, let's call a cab and head for the bus station."

"Where are we going to go?"

"Chicago."

"Okay."

. . .

"Here we are in Chicago. How much money do we have left after buying clothes and bus tickets?"

"Less than $150."

"Let's save it for food. We are going to have to go to a homeless shelter to spend the night. It's starting to get too cold to be on the street."

"Officer, can you tell me where the nearest homeless shelter is located?"

"Keep walking straight ahead, and when you get to Lennox Street, make a right. It is on your right about halfway down."

"Thank you, sir."

"What the hell are you doing asking a cop for directions? He was probably shown our picture before he was sent out on patrol. Must have a short memory."

. . .

"What can we do for you, gentlemen?"

"We are homeless and need a place to spend the night."

"You will be the best dressed homeless persons we have had in the ten years I have been here."

"Don't let the new clothes fool you. We were walking down the street when a gentleman said he wanted to buy us some new clothes because ours were so bad. He took us to Kmart, and we picked out these outfits. Talk about being lucky."

"Okay, come with me. We have cots on the floor that you are welcome to for tonight. We expect you to be leaving in the morning."

"Okay, you boys need any company?"

"You'd better get your skinny ass out of here while you can."

"There must be more of these guys than we think! They show up everywhere. Look how many are in prison."

"Let's settle in so we can get an early start in the morning."

. . .

"What do you say we stop and have a few beers? We haven't had a drink since we were released."

"Sounds good to me."

"Look at that guy paying for his drink. Did you see the roll of money he had? I think we could use some of that. Let's wait until he goes to the men's room."

"What if he doesn't?"

"We lose our chance, that's all."

"He is getting up and heading for the men's room. What's the plan?"

"Roscoe, you walk up to him and sucker punch him and knock him out. We take the money and run."

"Wow, he's out cold. Take the money."

"Man, he has more money in his other pocket, too. He must have been waiting to make a drug buy."

"Help me put him in a stall. Take his shoes and pants off."

"Okay, let's put them in the trash can in the women's restroom and get the hell out of here."

"Grab a cab, and we'll head to the bus station."

"Where are we heading, Jarvis?"

"Someplace warm, like Los Angeles."

"Let's do it. Two tickets to Los Angeles, sir."

"The Los Angeles Express will be leaving in twenty minutes on Number 14. You gentlemen have no bags, correct?"

"Correct."

"So, get on board."

"Let's sit here in the front."

"It looks like this bus is headed for Mexico City with all of these Mexicans onboard."

"Well, look who is getting onboard? You two girls will want to sit in the front with us, unless you speak Spanish."

"Okay, guys. My name is Kim and this is Jennifer. I'm an actress, and Jennifer is a fine jewelry sales expert."

"Why are you leaving Chicago?"

"Our boyfriends started using drugs and became very mean. Mine slapped me, and I took what money he had and decided to go to Hollywood and pursue my acting

104

career. I made Jennifer come with me, and she is not happy about our decision and is not talking to me right now. What are your names?"

"I'm Roscoe, and this is Jarvis."

"Why are you leaving Chicago?"

"We just feel that Los Angeles would give us an opportunity to find a better lifestyle than we had in Chicago."

"Do you think I have what it takes to make it in Hollywood?"

"Maybe in horror movies."

"That was a mean thing to say to me, Jarvis."

"Jarvis was only kidding with you, Kim."

"Thank you, Roscoe, you seem to be the nicer of the two of you. I don't like mean men."

"Driver, look at all those buffalo out there."

"Those are bison, not buffalo."

"What the hell is a bison?"

"Ted Turner is raising thousands of bison to replace the beef hamburgers that you eat now. He has started a chain of bison burger restaurants. The bison burger is much leaner and healthier than beef."

"Okay, have you ever eaten a bison burger?"

"Many times on this run. They taste great. We are now stopping at McDonald's for thirty minutes for food and drinks. No food or drinks allowed back on the bus. If you want water, buy bottled water only."

"Would you girls like to join us for dinner?"

"Sure."

"Jennifer, please talk to me. You know God has a plan for us that was much better than Chicago."

"Okay, Kim, but you'd better be right."

"Good to see that you are sociable, Jennifer."

"I'm Jarvis, and this is Roscoe."

"I know, Jarvis."

"Okay, let's get back on the bus. Driver, do you have any blankets or pillows to help us sleep?"

"This is the Greyhound Bus Lines, not American Airlines 707, lady."

"Well, you don't have to be so mean. Why are all you men so mean? It gets you nowhere, that's for sure."

"Our next stop will be Las Vegas. We'll have a one-hour stopover for food and drinks. We have public restrooms in the terminal as well as a restaurant. Our next stop will be our destination, Los Angeles."

. . .

"Okay, girls. Here we are."

"Could you get our bags for us?"

"Sure."

"You don't have any bags?"

"No, we didn't bring anything with us."

"Let's grab a cab and find a hotel that we can afford."

"Driver, we need a hotel that is not the Hilton but not the ghetto, either. Can you recommend one?"

"Sure, I can get you a nice hotel for $100 a night. How many rooms do you want?"

"Two, one for the girls and one for us guys."

"Okay, let me go in and make the deal since I get credit for bringing you here."

"Okay, since you are getting two rooms, they will give you both for $1200 a week. Is that acceptable?"

"Yes, here is the money, Kim. Go in and sign in for us."

"Roscoe, I talked to the desk clerk, and he says that there is a large shopping mall about four blocks from here, and they have a Men's Warehouse where he buys his clothes."

"Let's get you boys a change of clothing."

. . .

106

"Sir, we left two gentlemen here, and I don't see them now."

"These are the two, Miss."

"Oh, I didn't recognize them! Great job outfitting them."

"Everyone enjoys our buy two and get one free. They should be all set for some time."

"Back to the hotel, guys, after we get something to eat."

"Jennifer and I have some money to help pay for the room, but we need to start looking for employment right away. Let's get the Los Angeles Times and see what's available. Jen, here's an ad for an experienced, high-end jewelry salesperson."

"Let me call for an appointment. Okay, all set for tomorrow morning."

. . .

"How did your interview go, Jennifer?"

"Great, Mr. Goldberg was really impressed with my knowledge of the jewelry business. He was surprised I knew how to do the pricing as well as when to negotiate down in price and still make a great profit. He offered me a good base salary and a great commission plan. He also offered me a good price on a one-bedroom condo he owns in Oceanside that is completely furnished, and he'll deduct the rent from my salary. He'll even pay the condo fee. You said God had a plan for us, but I didn't know it was going to be this good. I can move out at the end of the week. I'm going to ask Jarvis if he would like to stay at my place since I know you and Roscoe are spending a lot of time together. I really like Jarvis, and a good man is hard to find. He told me that he will have a hard time finding employment because he was arrested on a felony auto theft charge when he was young and had to do prison time, but we will see how things work out."

"Roscoe, I bought the paper that has all the film auditions listed. Listen to this. There are auditions for the part of an African-American woman playing the supporting role in a new Spike Leeds movie. Would you like to go with me to the audition?"

"Sure, Kim."

. . .

"So, you are Kim. Kim, do you know that this part would be playing a prostitute trying to change her life in order to move up in society? Is that something you think you would be able to do?"

"Yes, sir."

"Okay, let's have a quick run-through with you reading a few lines with a fellow actor."

"That was really good, Kim. Can you come back at 4:00 this afternoon?"

"Sure, see you then."

. . .

"Roscoe, they want me to come back at 4:00. There were four men, and they were whispering something and then asked me to return at 4:00."

"Sounds really encouraging, Kim."

. . .

"We will have the three of you auditioning for Mr. Spike Leeds. Kim will be the last one to audition. Katherine is first and then Ashley. We will be filming your audition to see if you have any special appeal on film. Don't be nervous, ladies. Okay, I'm going to give each of you a full script to take home and study for two days. Guard it with your life. Come back at 10:00 Wednesday for the final audition. We will decide which one of you will get the part. You will see, by reading the script, that this is a large supporting role in the movie. So, it is really important that you do your best work on Wednesday. Mr. Leeds will watch the audition and make the final decision."

. . .

"Roscoe, I have read this script over and over. This is a part that was made for me. I just know it. What do you think about my going to the mall to buy an outfit that a hooker would wear, a short dress showing a lot of cleavage, high spiked heels, and a small purse?"

"I think that would blow them away. You could change in the ladies' room so that the other girls don't see what you're up to."

"Good idea. You will go with me. Roscoe, right?"

"Sure."

"I feel so much more relaxed when I know you are supporting me. Thanks."

. . .

"Okay, girls. We will be calling one of you at 10:00 a.m. tomorrow with the good news. Mr. Leeds wants to see the audition again on film to see who comes across the best."

. . .

"Kim, this is Spike Leeds. I have decided to take a chance on you for the part of Betsy in our new movie. Do you have an agent to represent you?"

"No, I don't, Mr. Leeds."

"Well, you will have to get one as we want to finalize this on Friday."

"Do you have any suggestions?"

"No, it would not be ethical for me to recommend someone. There are many agents listed online who would jump at the chance to represent you. Make sure you feel really comfortable with whomever you choose and that they will represent your best interests."

"Thank you, sir."

"Roscoe, we have to find an agent by Friday. I'm thinking Mr. Samuel Silverman looks like a good choice."

"Call him and see what he has to say."

"Mr. Silverman? My name is Kim, and I'm looking for an agent to represent me in negotiations for a film role."

"It is rare that someone calls who already has a part in a film. We would be more than happy to represent you. When do you need this done?"

"Today. I need someone to represent me on Friday."

"Where?"

"At Universal Studios with the production company filming Mr. Spike Leeds' new movie."

"Holy shit! Did you get the part of Betsy?"

"Yes, I did."

"Wow. Give me your address, and I will bring a contract over for you to sign since I can't legally represent you without it. My fee is 7% which is the standard agent fee. Does that sound okay with you?"

"Yes."

"I will see you later this afternoon."

. . .

"Kim, this is Sam Silverman. We are finished with the negotiations. They offered $5000 a week, I countered for $10000, and we finished up at a figure of $7500. If this is satisfactory with you, I will bring you back to the studio to sign the contract. Shooting starts Monday, and they project it will take six months to finish. Two months will be on location in Las Vegas. Be ready when I get there to pick you up. We are running close on time."

"Thank you, Sam. You did a great job. I am just so excited about getting this opportunity."

"Remember, you call me if any problem or conflict comes up. You never try to discuss and solve a problem directly with the production company. That is what I get paid for, and it keeps you from making any bad mistakes or making any enemies."

"Roscoe, you have to come to the studio with me every day. I can't do this without knowing you are waiting for me and supporting me."

"Okay, Kim. No problem."

"I have to call Jennifer and tell her. She won't believe it. I don't believe it."

"Tell her to tell Jarvis to stop by for a visit, and we will go out for a few drinks."

"Okay, Roscoe."

. . .

"I am so happy that the shooting of the movie is over, Roscoe. What do you say we go on a cruise to celebrate?"

"They were really happy with your performance, and they say the final editing of the movie is really spectacular. Okay, let's book that cruise!"

. . .

"Sam, this is Kim. We are back from our cruise, and we need a place to stay when we return to Los Angeles. Do you know a real estate agent who can find us a condo at a reasonable price? For the last two months, the production company paid for our hotel, food, and just about everything else, so I was able to save most of my salary."

"I will call Bob Hoffman, who is a friend of mine and a real estate agent, and see what is available. I also have one other possibility I will check on, but either way, I will get back to you in a day or so. I hear everyone connected with the film was really pleased with your performance."

"Kim, this is Sam. How would you like to stay in a gorgeous house in Malibu that is right on the ocean for a year, rent free?"

"You have to be kidding."

"No, my friend Bob Kinder, who owns Kinder productions, is leaving for a shoot in Europe. He'll be gone at least a year and wants someone to babysit his house. When I told him it was you, he was very happy because he already knew that you were given the part in Spike Leeds' new film. I will set up a meeting with him as soon as you return, and if you two hit it off, we should be all set."

. . .

"Hello, Bob. This is Kim and Roscoe, the couple I told you about."

"So, you're the actress that took the part away from better known actors. Spike must have seen something special in you. So, I guess Sam has told you I need someone to make certain that my home is well taken care of. If you are interested, I think we can settle this right now. I have to leave early next week, so the sooner you move in, the better. I want to go over the security system we have and introduce you to the cleaning staff that comes in once a week to do the cleaning. I also need to introduce you to my neighbors so that they will know that you will be staying here."

"We can be there tomorrow, if that's okay."

"Perfect. If I don't see you again before you leave, Bob, good luck on your new shoot."

"Thanks, Sam, I appreciate that. Oh, one more thing. I hope you don't mind parking your car in the driveway. I have both garages filled with my cars."

"No problem at all, Bob."

112

"Okay, guys. You will be staying at my home tonight, and I will be loaning you one of my cars to use to move into Bob's house."

"Do you have a valid driver's license, Kim?"

"Yes, but it is an Illinois license."

"That's fine for now, but I will take you down to the California DMV to get a new license so you can lease a car. After you are comfortable at Bob's, I need to go over two scripts you've been offered. One is from Mike Goldberg who has been patiently waiting for you to finish Spike's movie and is pushing me hard for a decision. I need you to come by my office to discuss this script as soon as possible."

. . .

"Good morning, Kim. Here is the script I was telling you about. Why don't I read the male parts, and you read your part to get a feel for the character?"

"Okay, let's do it."

"What do you think of the part, Kim?"

"I love it. It's not the main character, but I think I could really upstage some of the actors."

"Great. Let's call Mike now. Keep your hands over your ears."

"Mike, this is Sam Silverman. I am here with Kim, and she has just read your script, which I think is one of the worst I've ever read. Stop screaming, Mike. Kim just finished working for Spike Lee, and now you want her to do a low budget movie for you? Kim is a star, so if you want her, get ready to take out your checkbook because everyone knows you are the worst paying movie producer in all of Hollywood. Stop the screaming. We both know she is going to be the hottest property in Hollywood after the release of Spike's movie, so this would certainly help to make your movie a success. Okay, Kim says she is willing to do it. I will come by your office tomorrow morning, and let's negotiate the contract."

"This is going to work out great time-wise, Kim. Mike's move is scheduled for three months. The other film doesn't start until three or four months from now. We are no longer working for a salary. We want a fee up front which will be paid to a company we will start for you. We're going to ask Mike for $250,000 which is $20,000 per week. I can tell you exactly how this is going to go with Mike. When I say we want the $250.000 fee, he will jump up and say I am taking food from his kids' mouths, and he will have to sell his home and place his kids with relatives, and it will likely result in bankrupting his company. But, the man has more money than god."

"What happens after that?"

"I stand up and thank Mike for his time and start to walk toward the door."

"Then what happens?"

"One of two things – I either keep walking or Mike says, 'Why are you being so hard to deal with Sam, you're too sensitive. I didn't say I wouldn't pay it, so sit down, and let's draw up a contract."

"Well, I guess I will just wait for you to call to let me know if you kept on walking or not."

"Don't worry, this is not my first negotiation with Mike Goldberg."

. . .

"How is the filming with Mike going?"

"Just great, Sam. We should be finished in about another week, which is ahead of schedule."

"Good. We have to make a decision on another script soon, so let me know what you decide."

"Will do, Sam. Thanks."

. . .

114

"Roscoe, the movie release has been a great success, and I'm starting to get offers to do other roles. Sam says he has some good ones, but he's waiting for a big time budget movie from one of the big studios. Sam is sure it will be forthcoming."

"Kim, this is Sam. Have you heard the great news? You have been nominated as best supporting actress for the Oscars."

"You're joking! How many others were nominated?"

"There are three, plus you."

"This is incredible."

"Get a beautiful, expensive dress. You want to look great for Oscar night."

"Okay, I will. Thanks, Sam, you are a super agent. Roscoe! I have great news. I've been nominated for an Oscar. We get to go and sit in the front row. Isn't this great news? I have to call Jen and tell her that she and Jarvis have to go with us as guests."

. . .

"Oh, Roscoe, it's finally Oscar night. Do you think I can win over the other well-known actresses?"

"Sure, you were really great, and I think your chances are much better than theirs. You look great in that new dress."

"You look great yourself, Roscoe, with your beautiful suit."

"The limousine is here to take us to the Oscars. Let's go."

. . .

"I am here to present the Oscar to the best supporting actress, and the winner is – Kim for her portrayal of Betsy in the Spike Leeds' hit movie *Movin' On Over*. Congratulations, Kim!"

"I have so many people to thank. I thank Spike Leeds for taking a chance on an unknown actress and my agent Sam Silverman who is also my adviser and friend. But, most of all, I want to thank Roscoe, the love of my life, for sticking with me through everything that I needed. Stand up, Roscoe, and take a bow. Stand up, Roscoe, don't be shy."

"Linda, come here quick and look at this. See that guy right there waving to the crowd as if he was the Governor of California, and in the second row, right behind him, that guy right there next to the beautiful woman? Those are two convicts that escaped from the Indiana state prison."

"You have to be kidding. Are you sure?"

"Absolutely. I have to call our office in Los Angeles. This is Special Agent Jim Quinn from the FBI office in Indianapolis, Indiana. I am going to take the next plane out in the morning and am going to need your help in apprehending two fugitives in your area."

. . .

"Welcome to our FBI office in Los Angeles. How do you want to handle the take-down, Jim?"

"I'll go unannounced to the office of Sam Silverman first and have him call Kim to set up a meeting, making sure that she comes alone. We'll then go and arrest Roscoe."

. . .

"Mr. Silverman, I have some bad news for you and your client Kim. Her live-in boyfriend is a wanted criminal who was sentenced to 25 to life for murder. He escaped over a year ago with his buddy Jarvis. First, we need you to set up a meeting with Kim. Make certain she comes alone. Also, we need the address of Jennifer and Jarvis.

We do not believe that Kim knew any of this about Roscoe, so she won't be charged with harboring criminals and contributing to their welfare. We will arrest Roscoe and have him flown back to Indiana right after we arrest him and Jarvis. This should not reach the tabloids unless it's leaked from your end."

"Kim, this is Sam. I need to see you this morning. I'm sorry I didn't call you sooner, but I just realized that we have to answer some of these film offers by tomorrow. We need to make some decisions today. Can you meet me in my office this morning? Please come alone as we may have to leave the office and visit some studios."

"Give me an hour, and I'll be there, Sam. I'm excited to see what offers you have. Great work."

"I know you're not looking forward to what we have to do, Sam. We can't book a convicted murderer on a commercial flight, so we have a small charter plane ready to fly back to Indiana. Thanks again."

"Here is Jarvis's address. Arrest him and bring him into the office to wait for Roscoe, and we will get them out of Los Angeles right away."

. . .

"Roscoe, nice of you to answer the door. I'm FBI agent Jim Quinn from the Indianapolis office."

"Good to see you."

"Do you know why I'm here?"

"Hell, yes, I know why you're here."

"I'm here because you are a really stupid person, Roscoe. What did you think would happen when 14 million people were watching you stand up and wave to the crowd?"

"I had to take a gamble that Kim would not win and then the cameras wouldn't be on me."

"But, she did win, Roscoe."

117

"I didn't stand up the first time, but when she said it again, I couldn't ruin the best day of her life. I knew it was over for me."

"I have to give you credit. You had a great run. But, now you can say goodbye to the good life."

The Susan Britton Murder

My name is Bill Simmons, and I'm a senior homicide detective with the Boston, Massachusetts Police Department. One day, the chief called me into his office and asked me if I would be interested in solving a murder that was committed in Cedarwood, New Hampshire over a year ago. Their police department had asked us to send an experienced investigator to take over the investigation. They would pay all expenses plus my salary. The case had gone cold, and they had no leads that were viable.

It seemed strange that a young college graduate working for her father in his import business would be shot to death with two 22 caliber bullets to her head while sitting in her car. That sounded more like an execution style murder than anything else. Robbery was not the motive, so finding out why she was killed wouldn't be easy.

It was my decision to go ahead and investigate this case that changed my life. Realizing that I would be gone for some time, I packed all my belongings and cancelled my apartment lease with plans to rent an apartment at my new location.

Like the chief said, it was a two hour ride up Route I93, and I arrived in a very rural town that was beautiful and picturesque. I checked in with the police chief who told me I would be assigned a new, young detective named Jeff Wyatt who would assist me in finding a new apartment and also be my guide and take me wherever and whenever I wanted to go. He was familiar with the case file and would discuss all past details of the case with me. I had access to all police personnel and could ask any questions I might have as to what they did in their personal involvement in the investigation.

119

My first thought was that maybe there was some suspicion that someone in the town might not be as anxious to solve this murder as everyone else. I could be wrong, but my gut feelings are normally right on target. It would be necessary for us to interview everyone that Susan Britton had ever come in contact with. I think we should start with the father.

The father had only been to his office three or four times since the murder so that he could stay in contact with his employees, many of whom have been with his company a long time, as well as to check with the general manager and sign any necessary papers.

I noticed that his older daughter had taken a leave of absence from Smith College where she is an Associate Professor of Psychology. She is trying to help her father through this difficult time and has been seen around town doing all his errands. I probably shouldn't say this, but she really is a beautiful woman.

. . .

"I want to thank you, Jeff, for finding me the apartment in the Willis house. They seem like really nice people. I moved everything in this week and am all set to start our investigation. We will be meeting with Mr. Britton at his house this afternoon at 2:00, and while I'm asking the questions, I want you to watch the body language of his daughter Priscilla when I ask him certain questions."

"Do you suspect Priscilla might be involved in her sister's murder?"

"Everyone is a suspect right now, Jeff, until we figure out who the guilty party is."

"Okay, let's go to the Brittons' house."

. . .

120

"Hello, Mr. Britton. My name is Bill Simmons, and I am leading the investigation into your daughter's death on behalf of the Cedarwood Police Department. This is Detective Jeff Wyatt who is assisting me with this investigation. Thank you for giving us this time so we can familiarize ourselves with as much background information as you can provide to get us started. Let's start with what your daughter's responsibilities were at the export company."

"I guess the best way for me to start, Bill, would be to give you some background information first. Sue loved the business, and even as a child, she was always coming to the office, and we would give her jobs to do. She was always so proud of that. She worked summers for me when she was in high school and also when she went off to Babson College in Boston. She majored in business with a minor in communications. During the summer breaks from college, she would travel with me to call on our customers and attend conventions. She loved the interaction with our customers and had excellent sales skills."

"After graduating from college, we decided the best track for her was to start in the accounts payable section of the company where we actually had an opening. She would spend nine to twelve months in that position and would learn how we actually made money off of our accounts. After that, she started to travel with me to call on our accounts, the idea being that she would be taking over the business, and I would be retiring whenever she felt the time was right. Of course, we never got to do these things. It was difficult because her mother died a few years ago of breast cancer, so being together meant a lot to both of us."

"When Sue was murdered, I just fell apart and am now just getting my life back in order – with Priscilla's help. I intend to return to the business next week. That is about all I can tell you about what led up to this tragedy.

But, I'll be glad to answer any other questions you might have, Bill, so ask away."

"I have to explain to you, Mr. Britton, that this was not a random killing, in my opinion, and I am investigating it as an execution. There is only one reason that things happen the way they did with Susan, and that is the victim has information that would destroy another individual or information that would be detrimental to some type of illegal operation. Is there anything you can think of which would suggest your daughter could have had this type of information?"

"Absolutely not, unless it was something that happened at college before she came back to work for me."

"I don't think that is a possibility, but we will check it out. Priscilla, may I ask you a few questions since you are here? I understand that Sue's boyfriend lives in Boston and you, too, live in Boston. Did you ever have contact with him during the week, either via phone or visits, while Sue was in Cedarwood working? It's my understanding that Sue spent the weekends with her boyfriend, Henry Walton, in Boston."

"I never had any contact with Henry by phone or visits, unless they invited me to go out with them, which was very rare."

"Thank you very much, and I want to, again, thank you for your time and patience. We'll keep you informed if any major breaks are discovered in this investigation. I would appreciate it if you would keep this conversation private and not discuss it with anyone else."

. . .

"Jeff, did you observe anything about Priscilla's body language while I was questioning her father?"

"Nothing, other than that she seemed a little distraught when asked about the phone calls."

"Tomorrow, I'm going to need to find a local judge who will sign a warrant that will allow us to secure the phone records of both Priscilla Britton and Henry Walton for the last year, both cell and land lines. On Wednesday, we'll be driving down to Boston to interview Mr. Henry Walton at his apartment at 3:00. We'll be leaving here around 10:00 since I want to stop at the Boston police headquarters to visit my boss and some of my buddies from the homicide division. See you then."

. . .

"Good morning, Jeff. Ready to go to Boston? Do you mind driving down, and I'll drive back?"

"No problem, Bill."

"I got a judge to sign off on the warrants last night, and this morning I faxed them to the legal departments of both Verizon and AT&T. If they are satisfied with them, it should take no more than three to five days to receive a response, upon which I'll send them via overnight to your attention at the Cedarwood Police Department."

"I've already spoken to the chief and told him to be on the lookout for them and to make certain no one opens them in error."

"Good work, Jeff."

"Can I ask you a question, Bill? Do you really think there is a connection between Priscilla and Henry?"

"One thing you learn, Jeff, is never to start an investigation making assumptions. Also, you never want to find out at the end of a long investigation that if you had done the little things in the beginning, the time spent and the effort put forth could have been a lot shorter if every lead had been followed. All I wanted from Priscilla was for her to answer the question, and then I would check it out. She may have been telling the truth, but we will be certain with the phone records."

"One other question, what makes everyone so sure this was an execution? Couldn't someone make it look like that to throw everyone off?"

"I suppose that is possible, but we will find out when all the evidence is in. So, when we arrive at the Boston police station, I will introduce you to my boss, Chief Sullivan, who has a 90% success rate for solving crimes in Boston, much higher than the national average. He is a really great guy but just a little rough around the edges. It will be great to see some of the guys I worked with before becoming your partner."

. . .

"Park in the rear with the other police cars, and we will go in the back entrance. Let's say hello to all the guys first. Then, Jeff, you can have a seat, and I'll be back shortly to introduce you to the chief."

"Bill, how the hell are you? Finished with the investigation already?"

"No, I just started the interview process, and I came to Boston to check in with you and to interview the boyfriend this afternoon. I brought my sidekick, a young detective named Jeff Wyatt with me, and I want you to meet him before we leave."

"Who assigned this person to you?"

"The Cedarwood Police Chief."

"What do you know about him?"

"Only that he has a degree in criminal justice and has been on the police force for one year. Seems like a good kid, eager to learn."

"What would you think of my asking him to take a polygraph while he's here to determine if he's totally clean? I'll tell him that if we're not happy, we'll be sending him on an all-expense-paid trip to Mexico on one of those buses where he can sit on top with the chickens and snakes. Just kidding."

124

"I will say it's my idea, and he can refuse if he wants to."

"Okay, Bill, bring him in."

"Chief Sullivan, this is the young detective, Jeff Wyatt, that I was telling you about. He has done a great job so far."

"You like working with Bill?"

"Yes, sir."

"He's one of our best homicide detectives, and we want him back ASAP. There is one thought I had, Jeff. Since you are here, would you mind taking a polygraph? It would only be five or six questions, just so I can be certain you are only on our team."

"Do you think I'm some kind of plant that would do something to interfere with the investigation?"

"Jeff, let me explain myself to you. I don't have the luxury of thinking either way. We have our own detectives and policemen taking polygraph exams to determine if they have been corrupted, mainly by money. You can certainly say that you don't want to take the test, and that will be okay."

"Okay, Chief, I'll take the test."

"Great, Jeff. Bill will tell the examiner what questions to ask since he is more familiar with the case. Go with Bill, and he will tell you when to come into the examination room. See you after the test."

"Jeff, my name is Frank Hayes, and I'll be asking you a few questions regarding the Susan Britton murder. Did you kill Susan Britton?"

"Absolutely not."

"Do you have any suspicions of who might have killed Susan Britton?"

"No."

"Have you been asked by anyone in your police department to keep them informed of the investigation without Bill Simmons' knowledge?"

"Yes."

"Have you fulfilled such a request?"

"No."

"Who would you be reporting this information to?"

"The police chief."

"Will you be reporting this information to the police chief in the future?"

"No."

"If asked, what would your response be?"

"Nothing new to report, and Bill Simmons told me that he would be responsible for updating you."

"So, do you feel your loyalty is to Bill Simmons or to your boss, the Chief of Police?"

"Bill Simmons, and I will do everything to have his back."

"Okay, I'll send this down to Chief Sullivan, and I'm sure he'll go over it with you and Bill."

"Come on in, Jeff. Let's go over your transcript. I have only one question for you. When were you going to tell Bill about the chief's request to report any new information in this case directly to him?"

"I wasn't going to tell him because I wasn't going to comply with the request."

"Okay, then, this will be Bill's call on whether to keep you or have you replaced. Gentlemen, I've got to get back to work. Bill, keep in touch and let me know if you need any assistance, and we'll be right there with it. Nice to meet you Detective Wyatt."

. . .

"Okay, Jeff. We still have time to grab something to eat before we interview the boyfriend. He lives in an upscale apartment downtown, so let's find a parking garage first and have lunch."

"It's an easy walk from this parking garage to a restaurant I know in the North End called Lorenzo Brothers, better known as LB's, where Whitey Bulger and his gang, as well as other Mafia figures, ate quite often."

"Order up, and we'll discuss how we want to handle the questioning of Henry Walton. I will ask most of the questions, but when we are about to leave, I will say that I'm finished unless you have more questions. At that time, hit him with the question about whether he and Priscilla spent much time on the phone, met each other or texted each other during the week. I'll watch for any changes in his body language, and while you're asking the question, it is important that you look directly into his eyes. We will, of course, find out when we get back to see the records that show whether he is telling the truth."

"His apartment is in the Tremont Building, which is where some of the Celtics also stay, and it's very expensive. He has to be making a good buck to afford that apartment."

. . .

"We are here to see Mr. Henry Walton."

"I will let him know that you are here, Mr. Wyatt and Mr. Simmons. He said to go right on up. Take the elevator to the 18th floor and make a left. 1846 is on the right side of the hallway."

"Mr. Walton, let me introduce myself. I'm Bill Simmons, and this is Jeff Wyatt. As you know, we are detectives working the murder of Susan Britton who, I understand, was your girlfriend. We have been told that you were at home all day on the day of the murder. Is that correct?"

"Yes, sir."

"We also understand from Sue's father that you did not attend her funeral. Is that correct?"

"Yes, sir. I was too upset and knew that I would break down if I went."

"After the police verified your alibi, did they ask you any other questions?"

127

"No, sir."

"Can you think of anyone who might be involved or any reason that someone might have for doing Susan harm?"

"No, sir."

"She said nothing to you about anything she was worried about or that she was receiving strange phone calls or anything like that?"

"No, sir."

"Were you aware of what Susan's plans were for the future?"

"Only that she wanted to please her father and do a great job at his company."

"That meant she would be staying in Cedarwood. Were you okay with moving there if you got married? Did you plan to get married?"

"We did discuss our future together, but we would have had to find a place to live that was halfway between Boston and Cedarwood."

"Sounds like a good compromise to me, Henry. Well, I guess those are all the questions I have for now, unless Jeff has any."

"Yes, I would like to ask if you and Priscilla spent any time during the week texting, phoning or emailing each other."

"No, we were never that close. She only met with us when Sue invited her to town, which was probably about once a month."

"How would you describe their relationship?"

"Very close, even though they were eight years apart in age, and after their mother died, they became somewhat closer."

"Okay, Henry. Thank you. It's been a helpful conversation."

"Jeff, I want to stop in the lobby for a second and ask the desk clerk what number in the parking garage belongs to Mr. Walton. Sir, could you please give me the parking number of Mr. Walton's space? He told me, but I forgot it. Must be getting old, I guess."

"Number 105."

"Thank you very much. My, my, a new Mercedes Benz. Okay, Jeff, your next assignment is to find out what type of employment Henry has and try to find out about how much he is being paid in that position."

"Let's head back to Cedarwood. You want me to drive?"

"No, I'll drive."

. . .

"You did a great job, Jeff, in questioning Henry, and I couldn't help but notice that he was caught off guard by your questions and seemed to have a difficult time keeping his thoughts together. What did you think?"

"I agree. He was very nervous."

"What did you think of my boss, Chief Sullivan?"

"Do I really have to answer that? I was afraid if I didn't take the polygraph he might find an excuse to have someone shoot me."

"I told you on the way down that we can't afford to miss anything at the beginning of an investigation. The polygraph was totally his idea, but I'm sure you can appreciate his reasoning since none of us knows much about you."

"Well, I guess the next question, Bill, is do you want me as a partner? Someone who will have your back, as they say?"

"I am going to put my total trust in you, Jeff, until I find out that I can't, and that would not be a good position for you to be in. Let's get the investigation started. Let me know the results on Henry as soon as possible. Take tomorrow off, and I will be in touch on Thursday."

. . .

129

"Hello, Bill. This is Sam Britton. I was thinking that you might not have much going on here in New Hampshire and might be interested in coming over to watch the Patriots' game and get a good, home-cooked meal."

"That would be fantastic."

"Priscilla and I look forward to seeing you.

. . .

"Jeff, just wanted to touch base with you regarding the background check and financial check on Henry Watson. I already have the warrant for the financials."

"Do you want me to go to the bank or are you coming along? I realize you must be meeting with the president of the bank, and you'll want to keep it as quiet as possible."

"I think we should go together Monday morning. Next, I need to know, if at all possible, when the phone records will be arriving at the police headquarters. If it is Saturday morning, it would also be a good time to meet with the Chief, if he's going to be there."

"He comes in every Saturday until noon, and the overnight packages should be there by 10:00 or so, so that should work out. If there is any change, I'll let you know."

"Oh, one other thing. Where can I buy a good bottle of wine?"

"You will have to drive over to Fremont where they have a NH state liquor store. It's about a twenty-minute drive."

"Okay, thanks."

"Don't tell me you already found some female company in Cedarwood? Great work."

. . .

"Good morning, Jeff. Let's go in and see the Chief."

"The envelopes are already here, and I have them in the car."

"Okay. Good morning, Chief Belford. Do you have a few minutes so I can update you on our investigation?"

"Yes, sure, Bill."

"Well, we've just begun our interviews, and so far, we've interviewed Mr. Britton, his daughter Priscilla, and Sue's boyfriend Henry Walton. Our plans starting this week are to interview employees at Britton Import and Export Company. We'll keep you informed of any new leads we dig up. Can you add anything else, Jeff?"

"No, that pretty much sums it up."

"Two Fed-Ex envelopes arrived this morning that Jeff said you wanted. Was this part of the investigation?"

"At this point, Chief, I really don't think so. Have a great day, and we'll report in later."

.   .   .

"Jeff, let's take the phone records to my apartment and match them up to see if there are any numbers that may prove beneficial to our case. It might take some time to cross reference them. It looks like Priscilla didn't make many phone calls or send many text messages, so checking out her records should be easy."

"What is Henry's phone number?"

"Okay, let me go down the list and see if she called this number. It looks like Henry was telling the truth about not having contact with Priscilla."

"I'm really glad that is not the case."

"I have to go over to Fremont to pick up that wine. We can check Henry's records Monday for any unusual phone calls. We should hear back from Boston on his background check and examine his bank account. Take the rest of the weekend off and enjoy."

.   .   .

131

"Hi, Priscilla. Something smells awfully good. I brought along a bottle of wine for dinner."

"I hope you like lasagna, Bill."

"It is one of my favorites."

"Dad is in the other room since the game already started, but no talk about the investigation, please."

"I promise, Priscilla."

. . .

"This was a really great evening, Priscilla, and I can't tell you how much I enjoyed it."

"I know from experience that it's not anywhere near as exciting as being in Boston."

"Yeah, but I am enjoying the slower pace and hospitality."

"That's kind of you to say. I have to admit that I liked it too, but after a year, I am really looking forward to going back to Boston."

"When you do get back to Boston, we'll have to get together sometime."

"Yes, maybe we can make the rounds of the Irish pubs."

"That's a date."

. . .

"Hello, Chief Sullivan. Did you have time to run the background check on Henry Walton?"

"Sure did, Bill. This guy is so clean it's suspicious. We checked Facebook and all of the other social media sites and can't find him on any of them."

"Okay, Chief, thanks for the help."

"Jeff, I just spoke to Chief Sullivan, and he says that Henry's background check reveals a squeaky clean record, not even a traffic ticket. By the way, he sends his regards to you, ha-ha."

"Let's take the warrant over to the bank and get a copy of Henry's bank transactions."

. . .

"We are here to see the bank president, if that is possible."

"Hello, Jeff. How are you doing?"

"Just great, Lori, and you?"

"So much for keeping our visit secret. Good morning, Mr. White. I hope we are not keeping you from your work. This should only take a short amount of time. We have a warrant for the bank records of Henry Walton whose account is in the Boston office, but we were informed that as a branch of the same bank, you could pull up his records."

"No problem, Bill. How are you doing, Jeff? My daughter and Jeff were in the same high school class."

"We would appreciate it if you did not mention this visit to anyone else."

"Understood, Bill. Here is the printout. Hope you find what you're looking for. I also hope you solve this case."

. . .

"Let's go back to my apartment and go over the bank and phone records and see if we can find anything that ties Henry to this murder."

"Well, Henry certainly makes enough money to afford his apartment and car. These are all direct deposits from his company, and there are no cash deposits or any other deposits."

"His phone records show a lot of phone calls from Britton Export and Import, which must have been Susan calling him from work. Also, he makes a lot of calls back to the same number. The rest of the calls are single numbers and not any calls to the same number more than once."

"Looks like we can eliminate Henry from our list, Bill."

"You really think so, Jeff? By the way, I got to know Priscilla and her father very well after having dinner with them and watching the Patriots' game on Sunday."

"Oh, that's why you needed the bottle of wine?"

"Very observant. I can see you have a great future as a detective."

. . .

"Okay, time to start our interviews with the Britton Import and Export employees. Hello, Mrs. Ortega. My name is Bill Simmons, and I'm working with Detective Jeff Wyatt of the Cedarwood Police Department. We're investigating the Susan Britton murder. We would like to have the opportunity to ask you a few questions if you could find the time for us."

"I would be glad to answer any questions you might have, but I would prefer doing it somewhere outside this facility. If you could come by my home around 7:00 p.m. tonight, after my husband leaves for his bowling league game, that would work."

"Sure, we'll see you then."

"Do you need my address?"

"No, Jeff Wyatt knows where you live. Thank you."

. . .

"I know you were very close to Susan, and she probably confided in you after her mother died."

"Yes, she did. We had a very close relationship ever since she was a young girl and would come to work with her dad and play in the office."

"Her father told us what his future plans for Susan were, as far as the company was concerned. Did she confide that information to you?"

"Yes, she did since I was the one she would be reporting to as she carried out the different office responsibilities."

"I hate to ask you this question, but can you think of any reason anyone would want to harm Susan?"

"I really can't."

"Are you sure she didn't mention anything that was troubling her or that she was having any difficulty with?"

"She did come to me with a problem about paying an invoice to Atlas Customhouse Brokers, and for some reason, she went into the receiving database and could not find where a container had been entered as being received at our facility. She then went back and checked previous invoices and found that two more that had already been paid had not been entered into the database as having been delivered to our facility. I told her this was not something I could explain and that the general manager could straighten it out. I thought maybe the containers went directly from Portsmouth to a distributor. I really didn't know. I recommended she take it directly to their general manager for resolution."

"Did she do that?"

"I asked her several days later whether it had been resolved, and she said the general manager was still working on it."

"Would you know who approved the invoices for payment?"

"The general manager."

"Any questions, Jeff?"

"Only one, Mrs. Ortega. Did Susan ever have any visitors come by the office to see her?"

"Only her boyfriend Henry. He would meet her for lunch and sometimes wait until she finished work, but no one else."

"Mrs. Ortega, I have to ask you, please do not discuss this conversation we've had with anyone else. Will you do that?"

"Of course. I wouldn't want to interfere with your investigation."

"We will be leaving now, and again, thank you for your time."

"Jeff, I'm not sure what our next move should be, but I will contact you in the morning after I think about this missing container thing. Thanks for the ride home."

. . .

"Good morning, Jeff. I have decided that our next interview will be with Atlas Customhouse Brokers. Are you ready to make the drive this morning? Okay, good. Pick me up as soon as you are ready."

"Did you make an appointment with Atlas, Bill?"

"No, we will take our chances and just drop in. We have to be careful about how we try to get this information from him and not raise any alarms, but we will have to tell him we are investigating Susan's murder."

"Understood, Bill."

"I need to call Mrs. Ortega now and get the three container numbers billed for by Atlas but never delivered to Britton Import and Export.

"Good morning, Mrs. Ortega. Bill Simmons here. I need to ask you for the three container numbers that Susan had questions about. Okay, please call me back as soon as you can. Oh, one other question, did the Cedarwood police ever contact you regarding Susan's murder? No one ever contacted you? Thanks, Mrs. Ortega."

"Jeff, why do you think your police department never contacted these Britton Import and Export employees during their investigation?"

"I don't really know, Bill."

"What were you doing during their investigation?"

136

"As you know, I'm the only detective, outside of the Chief, to do any investigations, and I was handling breaking and entering arrests and marijuana possession. As you know, I have to drive to Concord every time we have an arrest and have them booked there. We have three part-time volunteer policemen that handle traffic stops, domestic disputes, etc. That left only the Chief to handle Susan's investigation."

"Well, here we are. Let's go in. We would like to talk to Jim Atlas, please."

"Jim, there are two gentlemen here who would like to talk with you."

"Send them in. I'm Jim Atlas, and you are?"

"Bill Simmons, and this is Jeff Wyatt. We are investigating the Susan Britton murder, and we certainly don't think you had anything to do with it, but I just wanted you to walk me through how the process works once a container is offloaded from the ship. I hope you don't mind doing that."

"No, not at all."

"Can we start after the container is offloaded? What is the next step?"

"I have the invoices faxed to me from the shipper, and once the container is here, I prepare the necessary documents to have the shipment cleared through customs. I then present them to customs and have them sign off, and then I call the general manager Paul Smith, as I have done for the last ten years, and advise him that a container is ready for pickup. After that, he sends a driver to pick up the container. The driver stops in my office to pick up the documents and goes down to the dock and takes possession of the container."

"When the driver comes in, Jim, does he show you any identification?"

"We make a copy of each driver's license and keep it on file for each container picked up."

"If I were to give you three container numbers, could you give me a copy of the driver's license for my files?"

"Sure."

"Here are the three container numbers."

"Okay, I will be right back."

"It seems that all three were picked up by the same driver, Roberto Santiago. I will make you a copy of the driver's license. May I ask why you want this information?"

"I do have another question, Jim. How often does customs inspect the actual contents of each container to verify if they are exactly what the invoice calls for?"

"It's been at least three years since any of our containers has been inspected. It really is like a family here as far as trust is concerned. I know all of the customs inspectors, and since we have been bringing in these same containers for years, they trust that what we say is in the container is actually in it. We are a small port authority, and customs doesn't have nearly enough agents to inspect all the containers."

"Anything else I can do for you, Bill and Jeff?"

"I had dinner and watched the game with Sam Britton on Sunday. He asked me to send you his regards and to tell you he is coming back to work very soon. He also told me to ask you if you would keep our conversation today private and not discuss it with anyone else. Can I tell him you will do that?"

"Absolutely, Bill."

"Okay, thanks for your time, Jim. It was really helpful to understand how all of this works."

"I'll drive back, Jeff, and I want you to get another warrant this time for back records and a credit check on the general manager Paul Smith. Also, call in the license number of Roberto Santiago, and let's get an address on him."

"Who is this judge who gives us these warrants without any questions?"

"I will only say that he is a relative of mine, case closed."

"No problem."

. . .

"Jeff, what did you find out?"

"Bad news, that driver's license is a fake, so there goes another lead down the toilet."

"Well, we do know what he looks like if we ever run into him."

"Call me tomorrow when you have the warrant, and I think this time you should go to the bank by yourself since everyone there seems to be one of your relatives. Make sure you emphasize to Mr. White about not divulging any of this to anyone else."

"Will do. Call you after I have the bank statement and credit report."

. . .

"Good morning, Bill. I have the bank records and credit report on Paul Smith, and I think you will be really surprised at the findings. I'll meet you at your apartment in about thirty minutes."

"Come in, Jeff, and let's see what we have. Wow, I would be more worried about Mr. Smith stealing from the company than anything else. He is overdue thirty days on his kids' school loans, mortgage payment, and credit cards. His bank account is down to less than $800 even though between his wife's salary as a nurse and his salary they are making close to $100,000 a year. Mr. Smith certainly doesn't seem to be involved in any way."

"Another dead end, Bill. We're not making very good headway, so far, with any viable suspects."

. . .

"Mr. Smith, this is Bill Simmons, and I would like to set up a meeting with you to ask a few questions regarding Susan Britton. Can that be arranged for today? Okay, good, we'll be there at 4:30 after most of your employees have left the premises."

"I understand that Susan Britton came to you with a concern she had about some missing containers from Columbia Chocolate. It seems you were billed by Atlas Customhouse Brokers for clearing containers that did not arrive back at this facility. Is that information correct?"

"Yes, she told me that Mrs. Ortega advised her to bring the matter to me and that I would look into it. After explaining the circumstances, I told her I would look into the problem and get back to her ASAP. I then called Mr. Alvarez at Columbia Chocolate and advised him of our problem, and he said he would look into the matter and call me back, which he did. His explanation was that these three containers belonged to another company, but since they had never shipped any containers to Portsmouth other than to Britton, the shipping clerk just assumed they were for us, and he apologized for the mix-up, told me to bill him for the Atlas charges for clearing these shipments, and told me he would see to it that they were paid for immediately. I explained this to Susan who did not seem satisfied with the answer and stated that she thought we should bring this up with her father upon his return."

"Do you know if she discussed this with anyone else other than Mrs. Ortega?"

"I don't know who it would be."

"One other question, Paul. How do you find out that a container is ready for pickup?"

"Jim Atlas calls me, and I arrange to have the container picked up."

"No one else could have gotten this call?"

"No, if I'm not here for some reason, Jim leaves the information on his voicemail."

"If Britton didn't pick up the container, who do you think did?"

"I really have no idea. I would suggest you contact Mr. Alvarez at Columbia Chocolate as it was his customer the shipment was consigned to."

"Thanks again for your time, Paul. It has been very helpful."

"Jeff, how would you like to have the rest of the weekend off to take a breather and relax a little? I have to go back to Boston to testify for the prosecution in a murder trial that I investigated over a year ago. I'm never sure when this happens when I will be called and whether I might be recalled by the defense at a later date. I will keep you informed."

"Wow, this is great timing. Some of my college buddies are going to meet in Miami Beach this weekend, and I think I'll go."

"Great, Jeff."

. . .

"Priscilla, this is Bill Simmons. How are you doing?"

"Great, Bill."

"I have a favor to ask of you. Do you still have that apartment in Boston?"

"Yes, I do."

"Do you think I could use it for three or four days this week? I promise I'll sleep on the couch and keep it neat and clean."

"Sure, Bill. Stop by to pick up the key."

"Thanks a lot."

"Chief Sullivan, Bill Simmons here."

"I know who the hell you are, and it sounds like trouble."

"I need to meet with you tomorrow morning, if at all possible. I need your advice on my next move and to bring you up to date on the investigation."

"8:30 sharp, Bill."

"Great, see you then."

. . .

"Good evening, Chief."

"Don't be a smart-ass, Bill."

"The freaking traffic to Boston in the morning is murder."

"I'm going to tell the Mayor we need another tunnel – this time with four lanes."

"Where are you going to get the money for the tunnel? Teddy has left us. Ted Kennedy is dead."

"Probably was a bad idea anyway. Speaking of bad ideas, I'm sure you have one, right?"

"You're going to love this plan I've put together. We now know that Susan Britton discovered three shipping containers that were consigned to Britton Import and Export after being cleared through customs and were picked up by someone else. We were unable to determine who was the actual consignee. The driver who picked up the containers used a fake driver's license, so that doesn't help us. So, I need to go to Bogota, Columbia and talk to the shipper, Columbia Chocolate, and try to find out some of these answers from a Mr. Alvarez without his being aware that I'm investigating Susan Britton's murder. Here is my new business card. Notice the name, John Wilson, 121 Biscayne Blvd., Miami, Florida. The telephone number is for a prepaid cell phone I purchased that accepts international calls. What do you think of my strategy?"

"Like I said, Bill, you have some really bad ideas, and this one is at the top of the list."

"I'm leaving early tomorrow morning on a direct flight to Bogota. I'm staying at the airport hotel tonight. I plan on making it a one day turn around, so I'll be back tomorrow night."

"Remember, John, your passport and tickets are in your real name. You might want to find a way to hide them in an airport storage unit. This is really not a good plan."

"Thanks for your advice. On my business card, my title is international sales consultant. I'm going to tell Mr. Alvarez that I'm handling Mr. Britton's accounts until he gets back on his feet."

"Let's hope he believes you."

. . .

"Mr. Alvarez, it was kind of you to see me on such short notice. I really appreciate it and so does Mr. Britton. I'm calling his accounts just to let them know that everything is still working fine. I understand that there was a little mix-up with some containers that were consigned to Britton Import and Export but belonged to someone else."

"Yes, there were four containers that we sent to them in error, but it is all straightened out now."

"Good, I also wanted to see if you would have any interest in my talking to clients about buying your products. We can work out a commission fee that would be agreeable to both of us."

"Sounds good to me, John."

"I would appreciate your showing me around your operation so that I can get a better feel for exactly what it is you do and get current information for our future clients."

"Of course, come with me."

"Well, you certainly have an impressive operation going on here."

143

"This is the end of the line, our shipping department."

"Mr. Alvarez, we have a problem on Line 3. Can you please check it out?"

"Excuse me, John. I will be right back."

"How many containers do you guys ship out in a day?"

"Normally five. This one's headed for Boston in a few days."

"Sorry for the interruption, John."

"No worries. I'll let you get on with your day. Thanks for the tour."

"You're welcome. Thanks for stopping by."

. . .

"Chief, I just left the Columbia Chocolate factory and all went well, but I need you to contact the DEA in Boston and set up a meeting today with the DEA supervisor here in Bogota. Can you do that?"

"Yes, I can arrange it if it's that important."

"It is, Chief. Have him call my prepaid cell phone number that can't be traced. It's on the business card I left with you. Many thanks, Chief."

. . .

"Hello, Bill. This is Jorge Marino from the DEA, Bogota office. You wanted to set up a meeting with me."

"Yes."

"Where are you now?"

"At the Columbia Chocolate factory."

"Do you have a rental car?"

"Yes."

"Stay put and I will send someone who will accompany you to a safe location. Give me the description of the car and the license plate number. Keep your doors locked until you receive a phone call

144

that someone is approaching your car. Let him in, and we'll proceed from there."

. . .

"I am Jorge Moreno. What is so urgent that we had to meet today? I understand from Boston that you are a detective investigating the murder of a young woman murdered in New Hampshire. What is the connection to Columbia Chocolate?"

"She discovered that three containers from Columbia Chocolate were consigned to her company and cleared by her customhouse broker, but the containers were picked up by someone else. I believe these containers had cocaine mixed in with the cookies, and the reason they were consigned to Britton Import and Export was that someone knew they would never be inspected."

"Sounds like a great plan to me. Where do we come into this investigation?"

"Mr. Alvarez was showing me around the plant, and there was a container being loaded that was destined for Boston. I think that is the new route they are using. Do you think you could find out the container number and get the shipping information as the container is loaded onto the cargo ship and advise your office in Boston to intercept and inspect it to make sure we're correct in our assumption?"

"That's no problem for us. We will follow through and advise DEA Boston. I hope you don't take this the wrong way, but your coming here was really a stupid thing to do. If you are right about the cartel using these containers to ship their cocaine, and they find out you're here, you are a dead man. They don't negotiate. They simply kill their enemies. I'm sure you know that from Susan Britton's death. She ruined a great method of shipping for them. We will drive you to the airport, and two agents will make certain you make your flight. There is a 10 p.m. tonight to Miami which we use to shuttle agents back and forth. I suggest you be on it. We will have an agent return your rental, and he will ride back with other agents. I do have one question. Why would they kill her after they already picked up the containers? That part doesn't make sense to me, but who knows. Okay, Bill, you're all set. Good luck with your investigation."

. . .

"Good morning, Chief. I just got off the plane from Miami because the DEA made me leave last night, so I had to take a connecting flight from Miami."

"What the hell was this DEA meeting about, Bill?"

"They are going to track a container from Columbia Chocolate to Boston, and when it arrives, the DEA will inspect it and make certain it has cocaine in it. They will then make certain that it passes through customs and follow it to the destination when it's picked up at the airport. We should then be able to know where their operation is based and move in to make arrests."

"Do you have a place to stay tonight, Bill?"

"Yes, a friend is letting me use her apartment in the city."

"Okay, keep me posted."

. . .

"Oh, Priscilla, I didn't expect you to be here. Am I still able to stay?"

"Yes, it's just that I have to go to Simmons on Monday and Tuesday to finish my syllabi for the upcoming semester, so I thought I would keep you company. I already purchased some food and wine, if that's alright with you."

"Hell, yes. Where do I put my suitcase?"

"Well, it's only a one-bedroom apartment, Bill."

146

"Interesting."

"Is it?"

. . .

"Great breakfast, Priscilla."

"Great night, Bill. So, do you know how you were chosen to help with this investigation?"

"No, I don't have a clue."

"Easy to explain. My father and your governor were college classmates. Both were majoring in business and had a lot of classes together, became good friends, and partied together, as I understand it. Your governor called my dad to give his condolences after Susan's murder and told him if he needed any help to let him know. My father, after about eleven months of no progress, asked the governor for help and was told that if the mayor requested it, he would send an experienced homicide investigator to help. Cedarwood's Mayor Andrews told Police Chief Anderson that you were coming, and I don't think he took it all that well."

"I've only met with him once to update, but I should do more to communicate with him when I get back. Okay, come over here and we'll move on to more pleasant topics."

. . .

"Jeff, I will be in Cedarwood around noon today and have some good news regarding the investigation."

"And I've been working with Chief Andrews the last two days, Bill, helping him catch up on his backlog. He wanted me to tell you he would like a meeting as soon as you return. I'm not sure what is on his mind. Can I tell him that you'll meet with him today?"

"Yes, I'll be there."

"Good afternoon, Chief Andrews. I understand you want to talk with me."

147

"Right, Bill. You haven't been forthcoming with me since you arrived here, and Jeff doesn't seem to be in on all that is happening in this investigation. Care to update me?"

"I really don't have all the dots connected as of now. What we have are a lot of pieces to the puzzle, but we are missing one or two pieces to complete it. I wish I could be more specific, but that's where we are at this point."

"Okay, Bill. Jeff has been working the last two days while you were in Boston helping me with a backlog of paperwork. I have decided that he should work with me for the next two or three weeks. He has spent enough time with you to familiarize you with the principals in this case as well as show you around the area. If you need anything, like a warrant, or are going to make an arrest in this case, we will certainly take care of those areas for you."

"Well, it is good to know, Chief, that you are still interested in solving Susan Britton's murder. Jeff has been a great asset in this investigation. If he isn't going to be available in two or three weeks, let me know now, and I will bring additional investigators from Boston to help out."

"My plans are for two or three weeks, Bill. I don't think additional help is needed at this time."

"Hello, Chief Sullivan. I have decided to take a break from this investigation for two or three weeks or until the container arrives from Bogota. If you want me to work during the break, let me know. If not, I plan to go back over this entire investigation from the beginning because I know I've missed some important clues that can solve this case. Okay, Chief, so we'll stay in touch. Oh, what is the name of the DEA agent who will be intercepting the container?"

"Dan Murphy. Hell of a guy. You two should get along."

"Thanks, and by the way, the Cedarwood Police Chief, Andrews, is still being a real prick. I haven't changed my original feelings about him because he's still not cooperating fully with this investigation. Anyway, talk to you later."

. . .

"Bill Simmons, this is Dan Murphy from DEA. I called Chief Sullivan, but he said to deal directly with you as this is part of your investigation. We contacted the customs supervisor, and he had the container seal broken so we could inspect the contents. We had our drug sniffing dogs enter the container, but they did not pick up any scent. We decided to offload the entire container and inspect every box, and finally, in the very front of the container, we found a large, wooden box which was painted exactly the same color as the inside of the container, which was great camouflage. We opened the box and found an arsenal of Russian-made AK47 semi-automatic rifles, loads of ammunition, and even some hand grenades. Since this isn't our area of enforcement, we contacted the FBI, and they are heading up an investigation along with the ATF and Boston police. The FBI told us to inventory the contents along with all serial numbers on the guns, which we did. We then reloaded the container and advised the customs supervisor to make certain that when the broker shows up, they clear the container so that it goes right through. That way, the FBI can track it to its destination. I realize this doesn't help your investigation unless the box is destined for a drug cartel operating in the U.S., which I doubt. Thank God we were able to find this shipment before it got into the wrong hands."

"Dan, is there any chance that we could meet somewhere and I could explain my theory about the cause of Susan Britton's death? I'm certain that I'm going to need your assistance since I've been going over

149

all of the facts in this case again and think I've solved it, but I'm just one piece short of the puzzle."

"Sure, let's set up a lunch for tomorrow. You pick the restaurant. How about Bertucci's on Central Street?"

"Sounds great. See you then. I'll be wearing a Celtics hat, so flag me down."

. . .

"Good afternoon, Dan."

"Hello, Bill."

"I'm starving. Let's order."

"What's on your mind, Bill, and how do you think we can assist you?"

"The reason Susan Britton was murdered was that she interrupted a Columbian drug cartel's operation. They were using Britton Import and Export to ship their cocaine in containers consigned to Britton although Susan didn't know it. Britton Import and Export had to notify Columbia Chocolate that they were being billed for custom clearance charges on containers that were consigned to someone else. Although they said it was a mistake made by their shipping department and they would correct the problem in the future, I realized that it didn't make sense to kill Susan Britton over it since the cartel had already received the three containers and were off the hook, as far as being found out was concerned. It was when I was in Bogota that the owner of Columbia Chocolate said there were four containers and not just the three. That meant that there was still one container still on route. The driver who picked up the containers had a fake New Hampshire driver's license, so that was a dead end. I'm convinced that someone in Britton Import and Export is involved. When I find out who that is, that's when I'll find out the information that will lead us to the actual drug distribution location. That is when I will need you to make the bust. I can give you

150

twenty-four hours' notice. Is this sufficient time for you to prepare to take down the operation?"

"Plenty of time, Bill. I hope you realize that these members of the cartel won't go down without a fight, so stay out of the way even though I know you want to be there. If this goes down the way you think, we will be able to turn at least one of them enough to find out who Susan's killer was."

"Keep in touch. You have my cell and home phone."

"Look forward to hearing from you. Good luck."

. . .

"Dan, I don't understand how or why they would be sending Russian arms in this container. There must be a better way."

"No, there isn't, Bill. You have to understand that the arms dealers need a drop off point that is safe where they can operate without a problem. There are landing strips all over Columbia, and they fly in, load the cargo into trucks, and take it to a warehouse for safekeeping in a remote location. The cartels all over South America have their own planes, and they fly in and land at a remote landing strip, pick up their AK47's and ammo, and fly out again. Some of these cartels own large ranches in their countries and have their own landing strips right there at their base. I know, I worked in Columbia for two years. The AK47 is the first choice of all cartels and of the jihadist movement. Every time you hear of a shoot-out with drug cartels or jihadists, it's with AK47's. The arms that were in the container were most likely purchased for cash by a third party, placed in a pickup truck, and driven to Bogota. Due to the size and weight of the merchandise, it has to be shipped in a container to avoid detection. They most likely bribed some dock workers at the chocolate factory to load the arms into the container. They probably paid them more

151

than they would have made in a whole year. It would have been done at night when no one was around. The money someone paid for the arms and the container full of product tells you how desperate they were to have these arms shipped to Boston."

"We'll have to wait and see who picks up the container to find out who actually paid for the operation."

. . .

"Hello, Bill Simmons. This is Rick Collins, your old buddy calling. How in the hell are you doing, Bill?"

"I'm doing great. How have you been? Still at the FBI or are you calling to come back to work in the homicide division?"

"No, I really love working for the FBI. The reason I'm calling is that I'm part of a task force which includes the ATF, DHS, and Boston police. Your name came up in our last meeting, and I told those present that I had worked with you for three years in the homicide division. They asked me to contact you to see if there might be some additional information you have regarding the arms shipment in that container that you informed us about."

"I really can't, Rick. It was my assumption that there would be cocaine in the container and not an arms shipment. Sorry, but finding it was more good luck than anything else."

"Okay, well, I'll pass that on. Can you brief me on what the status is of the investigation or is that confidential?"

"Since you are involved, I suppose it would be okay to brief you, as long as you don't discuss it with someone else."

"You know me; I can keep things very private."

"After the shipment was cleared through customs, a container truck contractor who works out of the Boston

Port Authority picked up the container and transported it to a warehouse in Woburn. He lowered the container to the ground behind the warehouse, and men came out and started to offload the products into a 22 ft. straight body truck which they had hired off Craigslist. It was one of those you-call-we-haul type operations, and they proceeded to take it to the recycling plant. We didn't bother talking to these two as we didn't want to have them thinking something strange was going on, plus we didn't think we could glean any useful information from them. The men then loaded the box with the arms into a white van which had been stolen in upstate New York. We followed the van, which ended up in Quincy, to a mosque where the box was removed and taken inside. They then drove back to the warehouse in Woburn."

"What did the men look like, Rick?"

"What do you think they looked like? Maybe long, blonde curly hair and blue eyes? You really should get out of the wilderness in New Hampshire and back to Boston before you lose it completely."

"Can you enlighten me on what the plans are going forward?"

"Our plan is to observe both the mosque and the warehouse 24/7. We figure that when the terror cell is ready to put their plan into action, they will go back to the mosque and pick up the box of arms. When they do, we will swoop in and arrest them and confiscate the van. We have purchased an identical van which we intend to back up to the warehouse door. We plan to bang on the door and hope they will open it since they should be expecting their men to return with the box. With the element of surprise, we should be able to charge into the warehouse and arrest all inside, as well as confiscate their cell phones and computers. Using the information from these, we should be able to track down other members of the cell. We are hoping that the public will not find out about this planned terror attack on Boston."

"What if things don't go well, Rick?"

"Well, it won't be a pretty sight, but we feel confident this will work."

"Call me when you get back to Boston, Bill, and we'll go out and have a beer and talk over old times."

"Will do, Rick. Good luck with your plan. I don't want to see you on TV."

"Hi, Jeff. I'm heading back to Cedarwood today, and during the last three weeks I've found some new information that should allow us to wrap up our investigation sooner than later. On the way, I'm going to stop in to see Jim Atlas, and then I'll be back later this afternoon. If you can drop by tonight, I'll bring you up to date on the latest."

"Okay, Bill, I'll be there tonight."

. . .

"Hello, Jim. I hope you have a few minutes for me. Good, I need the exact date that you told Paul Smith that the containers were ready for pickup. Let's start with the first one:

    Container OCL 3478CK – Jan. 12

    Container OCL 7855UZ – Feb. 1

    Container OCL 69076TS – Mar. 8

There were no other containers after that, Bill."

"Okay, thanks for your help, Jim."

"Bill, you're making me curious about what was actually in these containers."

"One last question, Jim. Who was the driver who picked up the last container?"

"Same driver, Santiago. I can assure you that the containers were full of Columbia Chocolate cookies."

"Thanks, again."

"Hello, Jeff. How did your three weeks with the Chief go?"

"Okay, no problems. What's up?"

154

"I want to go over the phone records of Henry Walton and see if he received phone calls on the dates that I received from Jim Atlas. First date, Jan. 12."

"Bingo."

"Feb. 1."

"Bingo."

"Mar. 8."

"Bingo."

"And Apr. 17."

"Whoa, that makes four containers, not the three we were looking for."

"Now, who would call Henry Walton from Britton four days after Susan was murdered? We assumed all of these phone calls to Henry were from Susan, which was a mistake. I know that they weren't from Paul Smith. It had to be someone else at Britton. We have to find out who that person is."

"How do we do that?"

"We have to go back to Paul Smith since he stated that he took the phone calls from Jim Atlas. We missed something when we interviewed Paul Smith. I'm going to see him tomorrow and go over the procedure he followed after he received that phone call from Jim. There has to be someone else who knows this information as well as Paul."

"Will you need my help?"

"No, but I think I will need you to get another warrant, so keep in touch tomorrow."

"Okay, Bill."

. . .

"Good morning, my name is Bill Simmons, and I would like to see Mr. Paul Smith if he is available."

"Go right in. Paul will see you now."

"Paul, I won't take up much of your time, but I just wanted to go over what happens when you receive a call from Jim Atlas that a container is ready for pickup. You stated last time that you arranged for the pickup. How exactly does that work?"

"Very simple, Bill. I email Roy Simpkins, the warehouse manager, with the container number and tell him to have it picked up."

"One more question, were you ever contacted by the Cedarwood Police Department regarding Susan Britton's murder?"

"No, no one ever contacted me, but they might have talked to other employees."

"That's all I needed. Thanks again for your time."

. . .

"Jeff, I need your help. I need you to get a warrant for the bank records of Roy Simpkins. Go to the bank and get me a copy. Bring it by my apartment as soon as possible."

"Will do, Bill. This is adding a new person to the mix. Do you think he is the one who made the phone calls to Henry?"

"Let's see what his bank records reveal before we start fingering someone for working Henry."

. . .

"Hello, Jeff."

"Bill, I have the bank records of Roy Simpkins. Are you ready for a shock? Take a look at February, March, and April of this year. There are $5,000 cash deposits in each of those months but nothing for January. He must have needed that cash to pay off some outstanding bills."

"Okay, Jeff, now it's starting to come together."

"Are we going to arrest him?"

"Not right now. I have to set up a plan with the DEA first, and then I will need you to get an arrest warrant since I'm not a New Hampshire resident. Keep all of this under your hat, and I will be back in touch with you when I have everything in place. I would like to do this on a Saturday morning when everyone is at home and relaxed."

"Okay, Bill. Call me any time you need assistance."

"Thanks, Jeff. I know I can count on you."

. . .

"I would like to talk to Dan Murphy. This is Bill Simmons."

"Hello, Bill, what can I do for you?"

"I've figured out who it was that was involved in the operation with the cartel at Britton Import and Export. It turns out to be the warehouse manager who kept Susan's boyfriend informed as to when to pick up the containers. Our plan is to arrest the warehouse manager early Saturday morning at 6 a.m. and drive him to Concord for booking and processing. My plan is to convince him to call Henry Walton and let him know he was arrested and is desperate for help in securing a bail bondsman. If I am correct, I think Henry will panic and drive to the operation site to talk to the person in charge of this operation. At that point, I will need you to set up the raid on this location. Are you with me so far?"

"Sounds like a good plan, Bill."

"Henry lives at Tremont Towers, his parking spot is 105, and his auto is a Mercedes Benz. We will put a GPS tracking device on his car so that even if we lose sight of him, we can still locate him. We will have an agent in the parking garage to watch his every move. I will put together twenty agents divided among three vans. They will have heavy duty arms and teargas canisters. We will also have an agent sitting in a judge's house ready to get a signed search warrant as soon as we have the actual physical address."

"This is a go unless we hear differently from you Saturday morning."

"Let's hope this plan works out. It will be a good bust for the DEA."

"Jeff, I need you to get an arrest warrant for Roy Simpkins. We will arrest him tomorrow morning at 6 a.m. and drive him to Concord."

. . .

"Here we are, Jeff. When we get inside, I want you to cuff him and read him his rights. Roy, my name is Bill Simmons, and I've been investigating the murder of Susan Britton. You are being charged under the Federal RICO Statutes for aiding and abetting in a criminal enterprise. This charge carries a minimum of twenty years in a federal prison. Roy, there is one way you can help yourself and possibly get your sentence reduced, and that is if you cooperate with us."

"What do I have to do?"

"You will have to testify at the trial against Henry Walton. You will also have to call him today, as soon as you are processed, and tell him you have been arrested and need help with your bail. Are you willing to do these two things? I will personally talk to the judge on your behalf if you cooperate."

"Okay, Bill, I will cooperate."

"Great, you'll get to see your kids before they are totally grown. I have to ask you, Roy, how did you ever get mixed up in this?"

"When Henry was waiting for Susan to get off work, he would spend time in the warehouse, and we got to be pretty good friends. One day, I was feeling down, and Henry asked me what the problem was, and I told him I was behind in my child support payments that had to be paid by the end of the month to avoid going to jail. He asked me how much I owed, and I told him $5,000. Later that day, he said he would give me the $5,000, and I told him I didn't know when I could pay him back. He said not to worry, that we would work something out. The next week, he invited me to dinner and said I didn't have to pay back the $5,000, and I could even make additional money if I would just make a phone call to him when a certain container number was ready for pickup. He explained that it had nothing to do with Britton Import and Export, other than that it was consigned to them for clearing through customs. I agreed, which was the biggest mistake of my life."

"Do you know, Roy, that if you had entered those container numbers in the receiving database, Susan would still be alive and you, most probably, wouldn't be going to jail? Okay, here we are at the county jail. We'll stay with you until you make the phone call."

"Dan, this is Bill. Roy Simpkins has agreed to call Henry Watson. Our plan will be going forward."

"Okay, Bill, we're on it. Keep in touch."

"Dan, Roy just made the phone call. Are you all set?"

"All set, Bill. Let's hope that it works."

"Bill, you were right. He is leaving the parking garage right now. We will keep you updated."

"Dan, are you still following Henry?"

"Sure are. Looks like he is going west and just turned on the Turnpike toward Worcester. Worcester would be a great distribution point with access to the Turnpike, I95, I93, and 495. You could be in New York in three hours and New Jersey in four hours with stops in Connecticut and Rhode Island."

"I want to meet you at the site if he goes there, so call me with the address."

"Will do, Bill."

"Bill, this is Dan. We are at the site. The address is 413 Dexter Highway, Worcester, Massachusetts. How far away are you?"

"About thirty minutes, I started out as soon as you told me it was Worcester."

"Okay, see you when you get here. We have the search warrant issued."

. . .

"Roger, you take nine agents and cover the front of the building, and I will take nine and cover the back. I'm going to bang on the overhead door and tell them we have a search warrant and to open up. Make certain you are not directly in front of the building but off to the left and right. Are you in position?"

"We are in position, Dan. Let's do this."

"Drug Enforcement Agency – and we have a search warrant for this building! Open up!"

"Three coming through the front door with AK47's."

"Start firing and stay down."

"Wow, three illegals that won't be collecting food stamps anymore."

"Dan, I'm sure you heard the shots. We just killed three of them. Steve took one in the leg, but it didn't hit the bone. We called for an ambulance. Hold on, I will call you back."

"Stop where you are!"

"I quit, I quit, don't shoot!"

"You are going to go back in and tell those in charge that if they don't open the back overhead door, we will kill everyone inside and won't hesitate to set the building on fire if necessary. Luis, tell him in Spanish. Okay, go!"

"Dan, we just had one of them come out with his hands up, and I sent him back in with the message to open the back overhead door or there would be big trouble for them."

"Be careful when the door comes up. We don't know what to expect."

"Roger, it worked, door coming up and I don't see any shooters."

"Nice work."

"Everyone down on the floor now. Hands behind your back. Cuff them and read them their rights. Well, imagine finding you here, Henry."

"Who owns the Lamborghini parked out front? What is your name, Señor?"

"Roberto Morales."

"You wouldn't be related to Juan Morales of the El Norté cartel out of Cartagena, Columbia by any chance?"

"He is my father."

"He is really going to be pissed at you, Roberto, when he hears that all this cocaine is going to go up in smoke. I have never seen this much cocaine in one place before. This is a great bust."

"Hello, Bill. Come on in. We have everything under control. We are going to start loading them in the vans and taking them to Worcester County Jail for booking."

"Hey, Dan. Come over here and check this out. I found this box hidden in some other boxes. It's a 22 caliber pistol with a silencer."

"Bill, what do you think?"

"This certainly could be the weapon that was used to kill Susan Britton. I can take it with me and send it to the NH Crime Lab to have ballistics verify that this is the gun."

"Okay, but I'll need you to sign it out on the inventory sheet."

"No problem."

"Thanks, Dan. I'm going to lock it up in my trunk for safekeeping."

"Dan, I need you to do me one more favor. Go outside and call this number. Give me about three minutes before you call."

"Henry, come over here for a minute. Are those cuffs too tight? Let me loosen them for you. There, how does that feel?"

161

"Better, thanks."

"So, shit, there goes my cell phone. What the hell did I do with it? Here, hold this for me, Henry. It's not loaded. Thanks. Oh, well, they'll call back. Let me put the cuffs back on, and you can go with the others."

"Okay, Dan, I'm leaving. Thanks again for all of your help. See you at the trial."

. . .

"Good morning, Jeff. We found a 22 caliber pistol with a silencer that I'm quite certain is the gun used in Susan's murder. So, before I return to Boston, there are two things I must accomplish. One is that I need you, as NH law enforcement, to take it to the NH Crime Lab in Concord and have ballistics determine if it is actually the weapon. You'll need to bring the two bullets that were taken from Susan's body to make certain this is the gun that was used."

"What is the second thing?"

"I'm working on a formal request to the State Attorney General's Office to have Chief Andrews removed for reckless disregard in performing his duties as a law enforcement officer. He swore an oath to uphold the duties of his office regardless of personal feelings, yet at no time did he ever interview any of Susan's friends, fellow employees or family members. Right from the beginning, he did not initiate a thorough investigation. The reason seems to be that Mr. Britton, who sits on the town council, voted against hiring Chief Andrews and convinced another member to vote with him. This was a public hearing, and Chief Andrews felt that Mr. Britton had embarrassed him in front of the Cedarwood community, even though the vote was 3 to 2 to go ahead with the hire. We'll see how far we get with this. Keep this to yourself whatever you do, please."

162

"Of course, Bill. You can tell me about the raid on the cartel site on the way. I'm disappointed you didn't take me with you, but that's okay."

. . .

"Chief Sullivan, good morning. This is Bill. I was just calling to let you know that I will have this investigation wrapped up in two weeks and will be reporting for work then."

"It's about time, Bill. You took six months for a six-week investigation. I would have had those Columbian bastards locked up long before now, and I wouldn't have had to fly out of the country to do it. We have a backlog of cases, and even though you're not very good at what you do, every little bit helps. Call me when you're coming in."

"Thanks, Chief. I miss you, too. Bye."

"Jeff, I'm going back to Boston as soon as I get all my things in order. I'm anxious to hear from the NH Crime Lab, so as soon as you get those reports, call me right away."

"Will do, Bill. It has been a great experience for me to work with someone like you. I learned a lot. Enjoy Boston."

"Thanks, Jeff. I will."

. . .

"Hello, Bill. This is Jeff. Have you gone back to work yet?"

"No, I start tomorrow."

"Well, I'm calling to tell you that you are batting a thousand. The ballistic report came back, and the gun is definitely the murder weapon that killed Susan."

"That's good news, Jeff."

"Wait, there's more. They found a set of fingerprints on the handle of the gun, and you won't believe who they belong to."

"Roberto Morales?"

"No, Henry Walton!"

"Wow, that's a surprise."

"One other piece of information for you. The mayor was advised that Chief Andrews was under investigation, and when she informed the town council, they suspended him without pay, and he immediately resigned and picked up his personal items from the office and left town. I have been appointed acting Chief of Police until they can find a replacement, the sooner the better. We need someone with a lot of experience to run this office as well as some additional manpower to perform all of the duties that are required."

"You would know better than I do, but I'm told that under these circumstances, they normally drop the investigation as his reputation is ruined, and he won't be getting any other employment in the law enforcement community."

"That's what normally happens, Jeff, but they also don't want to spend the money it would take to finish the investigation since he already resigned. As acting chief, you now have to do the following. Get an arrest warrant for Henry Walton, and take it to the NH State Attorney's Office along with the gun and the lab reports for both the fingerprints and the ballistic report. Tell them I will be available any time, at their convenience, if they need me. They will open the investigation, and it will be up to them to prosecute this case. They will also need to file a formal extradition order with the state of Massachusetts to have Henry brought back to New Hampshire for the trial. This can't happen until he is tried in Massachusetts for his part in smuggling cocaine into the United States. At any rate, good luck with your new responsibilities. If you need any help, give me a call."

. . .

"Good morning, Chief."

"I see you're at your old desk, Bill. Solving any murders yet?"

"I'm looking for the most difficult ones – the ones you weren't able to solve."

"Come into my office, Bill. Listen, I need you to keep next Wednesday night open. I'm arranging a dinner at a great hotel for you, Rick, Dan, and me."

"Will do, Chief. Who's paying?"

"Don't worry about it."

. . .

"Okay, let's all drink up and enjoy the evening. I didn't invite you all here because I enjoy your company. I was ordered to do so by the Police Commissioner. I have a few announcements to make. First, Rick and Dan will be receiving a special plaque from the governor's office, along with a special letter of commendation for a job well done. This will be sent to your superiors to be presented to you at a ceremony. The governor will be attending. Bill, you'll be receiving a promotion from detective to lieutenant. This was done by executive order for exemplary service given to your state."

"Don't I get a plaque?"

"You just got a promotion and pay raise, Bill. What the hell more do you want?"

"What special service did he do? All he did was give me the wrong information about a container. It was supposed to be full of chocolate chip cookies."

"In my case, he made a mistake and lucked into our finding a terror plot."

"I know, but it pays to be lucky sometimes rather than good."

"Chief, I would like to ask a favor if I could. I would like to have you hire Jeff Wyatt, who you met, to be an investigator in our homicide division."

"I can't, Bill. We have a hiring freeze on the whole department now. Have you already discussed this with him?"

"No."

"You'd better find a way to make this happen, Chief, or some of Bill's friends will call the governor, and you will be replaced by a woman from the traffic division."

"I do have a detective retiring in a few months. I might slip him in that slot."

"Bill, you and this Jeff guy aren't planning on getting married are you?"

"That's a homophobic statement, Rick."

"Just asking. You have never been married, and Jeff is single."

"Answer your damn cell phone, Bill."

"Great, and I've already bought the wine."

"That wasn't Jeff, was it?"

"Don't tell me he also gets the girl that he found up there in the woods."

"She's beautiful, highly educated, and a college professor."

"And she's from New Hampshire."

"No, she's from Boston."

"Show us a picture that you have on your phone."

"I don't have any pictures."

"I bet you have a nude picture of her."

"He won't show you a nude picture because she is probably covered in tattoos."

"What a turn on, seeing a nude, tattooed woman."

"This has gone on long enough. You guys should be charged with hate speech and arrested."

"This has been a not so politically correct conversation tonight."

166

"I'm going to give Dan's name to our sexual deviant division to look into."

"Let's leave before we all have to take a taxi."

"It's been fun guys, really. Let's go home."

. . .

"All rise for the Honorable Judge Gerard E. Murdoch, presiding."

"First, I want to ask the defendant if he willingly waves his right to a jury of his peers and will abide by the decision of the sitting judge."

"I do, your Honor."

"Let's begin the proceeding by having the prosecution present opening arguments. Are you ready Counselor?"

"Yes, your Honor, but I have a request to make. Since we are presenting our case to you instead of just making an argument, I would like to make a statement before I present each of our documents to you. It will save the court a lot of time. I have turned over to the defense all of the documents that I will be giving the court."

"Are there any objections from the defense?"

"No, your Honor."

"As you know, your Honor, the defense has requested to dismiss this case because Lt. Simmons framed the defendant. I will start out by providing you with documentation refuting the allegation."

"Okay, let's get started Counselor."

"Document 1: Here are the cell phone records of Lt. William Simmons that will prove that no phone calls were incoming or outgoing during the time of the warehouse raid.

Document 2: We have a signed statement from all of the DEA agents who participated in the raid that at no time did they see Lt. Simmons and the defendant alone in the warehouse.

Document 3: Mr. Daniel Murphy, who led the raid on the warehouse, is out of the country on an undercover mission, but we were able to get a sworn statement from him that reads as follows: 'Bill came to me with a box with a firearm in it and said he thought it might be the murder weapon used to kill Susan Britton. He wanted permission to have it placed in his possession so that he could send it to ballistics. I told him he had to sign out for it, but he could take possession. He then told me he was going to place it in the trunk of his car for safekeeping. The last I saw of him, he was heading for the front door with the box.

Document 4: These are the written reports from the NH Crime Lab that show the fingerprint comparison and also the firearm test to prove this was the firearm used to kill Susan Britton.

Document 5: These are two videos that we were able to secure from the parking lot garage at the defendant's residence. They clearly show that on April 13, the date of the murder, the defendant left the parking lot at 1:14 p.m. and returned at 7:36 p.m. This is so important because the defendant lied to Lt. Simmons during his interview stating that he was home all day and never left the residence.

Document 6: The defendant's cell phone records indicate that he did not take his cell phone with him on that day. He left it in his apartment. We do not know whether this was intentional or if he just forgot it.

Document 7: The defendant stated that he left to meet with Roberto Morales in Worcester. Mr. Morales will not testify as to whether this was a true statement or a false statement.

As you can see, your Honor, we have an abundance of evidence in this case. Our theory is that the reason the defendant killed Susan was that a fourth container was due to arrive in Portsmouth within days, and if

Susan discovered it, she would tell her father or, even worse for the defendant, call customs. He was told to commit the murder or the cartel would do it, which he knew meant he would also be killed. That is all we have for you right now, your Honor."

"Is the defense ready to present its argument or statements to the court?"

"We are, your Honor. In regard to the cell phone records of Lt. Simmons, we contend that he had two cell phones. There was definitely a cell phone ringing when Lt. Simmons handed the firearm to the defendant to hold, and he did so without thinking. As for videos from the parking garage, the defendant did not take his cell phone because he was afraid of giving away the location of the warehouse and knew that he could be tracked by the location of the cell phone pings from his cell phone. We believe that Lt. Simmons, who is engaged to be married to Susan Britton's sister Priscilla, has a personal vendetta against my client and would do anything to see him convicted of first degree murder. At this time, we are still in the process of getting verification from Roberto Morales that he did meet with the defendant on April 13. We will submit that as soon as we get it. That is all I have for now, your Honor."

"Okay, let's start the next phase by calling witnesses. The prosecution will call their first witness to the stand."

"We call Lt. Simmons, your Honor."

"Stand and be sworn in. Do you swear to tell the truth and nothing but the truth, so help you God?"

"I do."

"I have noticed that it is already 4:30. We are going to adjourn for the day and resume the hearing at 10:00 tomorrow morning. Court adjourned. I would like to have both counselors approach the bench. I would like to see you in my chambers. Follow me. I have listened to both sides, and I am wondering if there might not be a plea bargain that should first be offered to the defendant if the prosecution is willing. We could offer to reduce his charge to a second degree murder with a minimum of 30-40 years in jail without parole. What say you, Counselor?"

"I'll inform my client, and I will have an answer for you by tomorrow morning."

"Meet me back here at 9:30 a.m."

. . .

"Well, I see everyone is here. What have we decided?"

"Our client, Henry Walton, states he would agree to a 20-year sentence with parole privileges. This would be served concurrently with the 10-year sentence he is now serving for his cocaine smuggling conviction, thus giving him 30 years but with a chance of parole."

"We accept your plea bargain pending agreement by the Attorney General. I'm not sure he will okay this as this case is a slam dunk for us."

"Can you have your answer back by 1:00 today?"

"I can, your Honor."

"Okay, if the answer is no, then we will proceed with the sworn testimony of Lt. Simmons on the stand. Please ask the bailiff to come in here on your way out. Thanks again. Bailiff, tell the court we are delayed until 1:00 p.m."

"Yes, your Honor."

"Since both parties have agreed to the plea bargain, I am going to dismiss the jury and close this trial."

. . .

"Well, Bill, I'm so glad that this trial is finally over. I can't thank you enough for all the time and hard work you put into this investigation for my daughter. Did you have any idea that Henry killed Susan?"

170

"From the very first interview when he told me he did not attend Susan's funeral, I knew he either killed Susan or knew who was involved. It is my honest belief that if Susan hadn't met Henry, she would be alive today."

"I know you and Priscilla want to get back to Boston and live a normal life, so I'll let you go now. Any chance of grandchildren in the future?"

"We are working on it now, Sam."

The First Time

"Thank you all for coming. My name is Alfred Smith, and I am running as an independent candidate on a third party ticket. The State Assembly race for the second district of the city of Oakland and the towns of Baylor and Lewis are ready for a change. I think that my experience in business will help to bring back the economy if I am elected. I believe the public is ready for a change from the Democratic and Republican bullshit that we have been given over the last forty years. You have a copy of my bio. I will now open it up for questions. Please state your name and media affiliation."

"My name is Carol Dawkins from the Oakland Gazette. It states here that you are now employed by Walmart."

"Yes, that is true. I have just been promoted to Customer Service Return Specialist. They have graciously allowed me to work the midnight shift so that I can spend days and weekends on my campaign."

"All of your other work experience seems to be for fast food restaurants: Wendy's, Burger King, McDonald's, IHOP, and Arby's. What were your responsibilities at those companies?"

"I was always involved in the customer service area."

"Do you mean that you took orders as customers came into the restaurant?"

"That is correct."

"You received an associate's degree from Oakland Community College, but there is no specific major listed."

"That is because Oakland Community College allowed me to design my own degree. Instead of selecting one area of study, such as computer coding, I chose to take one class in each subject area so as to be well-rounded and able to converse on many topics. I was much more interested in being able to be a great communicator than anything else."

"Is it true you have been married four times and have four children, one with each of your ex-wives?"

"This is true."

"I know this is a personal question, but could you tell us a little about why you were divorced four times?"

"In each marriage, everything was going along fine until after the birth of the child. Then, the mother of the child, after about two months, became very hostile and had mood swings that tended to be violent. I understand this is common in most women. It is some kind of neurosis."

"Do you realize, Mr. Smith, that over fifty percent of the Second District voters are women?"

"Yes, I do, and I think more women should be involved in politics, and I hope many will become involved in my campaign."

"How old is your child from your first marriage?"

"I really am not sure. I think 17 or 18 or close to that age."

"I'm sorry that your four other reporters did not get a chance to ask me questions, but I have to leave now and get some sleep so I can report to Walmart at midnight."

. . .

"Mr. Smith, my name is Carol Dawkins. I want to ask you a few questions regarding your ex-husband as he is now running for public office. He claims you were rather hostile and treated him violently."

"Yes, that is true. I was mad as hell. Two months after Antonio was born, I was back working two jobs, and my mother was taking care of Antonio while Big Al was at home watching TV and drinking beer. I told him if he didn't get a decent job and help out financially, I would have to take Antonio and move back with my mother.

173

That is exactly what happened, and I kicked him to the curb. In our divorce agreement, he was to pay me child support, which he never did, so I never allowed him to see Antonio. To this day, he has never spent any time with his son who is now 18. I better stop there. I have probably said too much. Excuse me. Antonio! No smoking in the house! Antonio is on prescription medical marijuana for ADD and anxiety disorder. Some doctors say it was caused by Antonio not having a male influence in his life. I guess that is on me."

"Well, thank you, Mrs. Smith. It was a pleasure talking to you."

. . .

"Well, here we are at my second press conference, and I notice that all three of you seem to be anxious to ask some questions, so let's get started."

"Carol Dawkins from the Oakland Gazette."

"I know who you are, Carol. I read your hit piece on me in the last edition. What is your question?"

"As you know, I interviewed your first wife, and I was wondering if you could enlighten us about your second marriage."

"My second wife is from Zimbabwe. I was doing volunteer work with my church, and Towanda was one of three persons that the First Baptist Church was sponsoring in the United States. We hit it off right away and married six months later. Her English was quite good, which made it easier for us to communicate. It was only about two months after our daughter Jasmine was born that the neurosis kicked in, and I had to abandon that marriage."

"How old is your daughter now?"

"I'm not quite sure. I think about 13 or 14 maybe. That is all for now. I have to get ready for my job at Walmart. Thank you for coming."

. . .

"Mrs. Smith, I'm Carol Dawkins from the Oakland Gazette. I want to ask you a few questions about your ex-husband, Alfred Smith."

"I have remarried to a wonderful man, and my name is Mrs. Washington. My new husband has adopted my daughter Jasmine, and we are a very happy family."

"I am sure you are, but would you please just answer a few questions about your ex-husband?"

"What do you want to know?"

"What was the real reason the marriage failed?"

"Big Al, as he made me call him and I don't know why, had some kind of neurosis, and about two months after Jasmine's birth, he started to act crazy. The doctor told me that some men can't handle seeing their wife giving all their attention and love to another individual. I just couldn't handle his violent outbursts and mood swings, so I had to kick him to the curb. That is all I have to say. Please excuse me. I have to pick Jasmine up at school."

"Thank you for your patience. Goodbye!"

. . .

"This is my third press conference, and I notice that there are only two of you reporters this time. Who would like to start first?"

"Carol Dawkins from the Oakland Gazette."

"Yes, Carol, I read your second hit piece on me, and my Twitter account has been overwhelmed with responses to your article. Thank you for getting my name out there to many more people than I could ever have imagined."

"You're welcome, Mr. Smith. I wanted to know about your third marriage since there seems to be a difference between that one and your first two marriages."

"Why didn't I see that question coming? I met my third wife when she was working at a cleaning service that came in at closing time at the IHOP restaurant where I was working the late shift. She spoke very little English. She was from Bolivia and was sort of half-Spanish and half-Indian. She snuck across our southern border illegally and joined her relatives, who also had entered illegally through Mexico, here in Oakland. Now you can see why I am such an expert on immigration. I have firsthand knowledge of how it works, thanks to Margarita. We were married about six months later and had a daughter named Repita. That name was my idea. The same thing happened after Repita was born, another neurosis attack, and the extreme abuse and violent mood swings were just too much for me to take. But, she had her green card and was able to get a great job."

"How old is Repita now?"

"Repita should be ten or eleven. I'm not quite sure. Any other questions before we wrap up? Okay, I have to get back to knocking on doors, and I must admit that I have a very good feeling about my chances in this race."

. . .

"Mrs. Smith, may I have a few minutes of your time, please? My name is Carol Dawkins. I'm a reporter with the Oakland Gazette. Your ex-husband is running for the assembly, and I would like to ask you a few questions, if you don't mind."

"I can tell you this. He is a damn loser; that is for sure. No child support or any other help with Repita. He never could hold a steady job, and we were always on welfare. I finally got a good job at the Hilton Hotel and am now able to support Repita myself. I never want to see him again, and I can't imagine that a man with his limited intelligence would ever be elected to any office.

176

When I kicked him out of our house, he was drunk as a skunk and ranting and raving. That is the last time I actually saw him. I really have to get ready for work. So, if you will please excuse me, I must end this interview."

"Thank you very much, Mrs. Smith. I will find my own way out."

. . .

"This is my fourth press conference. I am disappointed that there are only two of you here. I guess the word did not get out. Anyone have any questions?"

"Yes, Carol, what do you want to ask me – as if I didn't know. I only have one marriage left that you haven't investigated. Your last column had my Twitter account all fired up, and I really must thank you for exposing me to all of the voters who didn't know who I am."

"I would like to know about your fourth wife and what went wrong with that marriage. I want to hear your side of it first."

"I met Desiree at a Lil Wayne concert. She had come to Oakland to visit her sister and brother-in-law and their family. We really got along well, and she decided to prolong her visit so that we could spend more time together. She was from Mississippi and had a very strong accent and, at times, was hard to understand. I wanted her to attend ESL classes at Oakland Community College, but she refused. Shortly after we were married, she became pregnant with Rocko. Again, I was faced with that damn neurosis that had been following me around through all four of my relationships."

"I would ask you how old Rocko is, but I will save you the embarrassment of not knowing."

"If there are no more questions, I will be going back to campaigning, which seems to be going quite well thanks to you, Carol Dawkins."

"I don't understand how that could be, Mr. Smith. All my stories have been very critical of you. How does that help you?"

"Most of my Twitter followers think that you, as part of the media, are biased and in the bag for the Democrat candidate. They feel like you have not given me a fair hearing and are really pissed off at you. Keep up the good work on your next story."

"This is my last press conference before Tuesday night's election. Results are in. I noticed, Carol, that you did not write a story about my last marriage. What happened? Couldn't find my ex-wife?"

"No, my editors felt that you were not going to win this election, so why waste another story that might help you in a rather bizarre way?"

. . .

"Ladies and gentlemen, the total vote count is in from Oakland now and, combined with the votes from Baylor and Lewis, here are the totals. The Republican candidate received 28%, the Democratic candidate received 33%, and the first time Independent candidate received 39% of the vote and is now our new State Senator. Congratulations, Mr. Smith. This proves that a revolution is underway and that the voters definitely want a change. There is no doubt about that. No one saw this coming. Is this the wave of the future? No one knows for sure, but let's sit back and enjoy the ride."

Fighter and Family

"I'm not going to the gym today, Arthur, as I'm leaving tomorrow for New York City for my fight in Madison Square Garden for the Heavyweight Championship of the World. I'm 36 years old now, and this will be my one and only chance to win the title. I have worked hard, you know, for this opportunity. It is hard to believe you are now 14 years old, son. All of the sacrifices you and your mother have been making to support me all of these years are going to pay off."

"The worst thing, Dad, was your never spending time with us. You get up at 5 a.m. and run five miles, come home, and get ready to go to work and then come home from work, eat dinner, and go to the gym. You do this every day and also spend your weekends at the gym working out and doing sparring with the other boxers. Why has this routine been necessary for so long?"

"A boxer must always be in the best shape possible as he never knows when a fight will be scheduled. Many times, you are given only three or four days' notice, and being prepared for a fight on short notice requires you to be in great shape at all times."

"I understand that, Dad, but I still don't understand what you are trying to achieve. We have a great, loving family, a nice house, and enough money from your regular job to spend more time as a normal family. I'll soon be in college, and even though I know you love me and I love you, I feel like I will look back and think I never had the opportunity to really get to know you or for you to get to know me."

"When you do get to college, son, and you realize you have the dream you want to follow and goals you want to achieve, then you will start to understand what I do why I do it. My dream is to put my family in the best financial position I can possible attain for them. Growing up dirt poor and not having enough to eat or shoes to wear to school is something you never forget, and I promised myself that someday I would be able to provide for my family all the things I did not have. I hope you don't think this is selfish or that I just have a big ego. It is not. I truly want to give you and your mother and grandmother a much better life than I had growing up."

"The kids at school always ask me why my father never shows up for my soccer games, and I tell them that you are in training, and when they find out it is because you are a boxer, they think that's really cool. When I tell them you are going to be fighting for the heavyweight title, they will be really impressed."

"I am going to make you a promise, Arthur, and I don't want you to tell your mother until the day of the fight. Ready?"

"Okay, let's hear it."

"If I do lose this fight, it will be my last one. My percentage from the purse of this fight will be enough to keep us financially sound for quite some time. I don't even like to think about losing, but after talking to you, I think it is important that you know we will have a more normal home life, and I am sure your mother will be extremely happy. If I win, of course, I won't be home for quite some time with all of the interviews and traveling that will be required. Let's hope I win so your friends will really be impressed. But, I promise I will make a special time each week for just the two of us to spend time together. I love you, son, more than you will ever know. Okay, let's head back to the house."

"Okay, Dad, I love you, too."

. . .

"I have all your clothes and personal items packed, and your manager called to say he will pick you up tomorrow morning at 8 o'clock to take you to the airport. He said to get a good night's rest and to eat a good breakfast."

. . .

"They are here to pick me up. I will call you tonight. Goodbye. Give me a hug, Arthur, and wish me the best."

"You know we are pulling for you, Dad. Mom won't let me watch the fight on TV, so call afterwards and let me know the results."

"Will do, Arthur. Love you guys. See you in a couple of days."

"Mom, the kids at school said that their fathers told them the champion has a record of 20 knockouts in 25 fights, and Dad has only 5 knockouts in 30 fights. They don't think he can win."

"Well, Arthur, I remember all the experts claiming that Muhammad Ali would never beat Sonny Liston for the heavyweight title in Miami, but when it came to the seventh round, Sonny Liston could not get up off his stool to continue. The experts aren't able to determine the amount of strong will and fight in the heart of a true champion."

"Well, that makes me feel a lot better."

"What did your father mean when he said, 'Tomorrow, Arthur, not until tomorrow?'"

"He has a message that I'm supposed to give you just before the fight tomorrow night."

"Oh, you can tell me now, Arthur."

"No, Mom. You and grandma will have to wait. I promised Dad, and I have to keep that promise."

"Okay, Arthur."

. . .

"Get the door, Arthur. That will be your grandmother, and she will be watching the movie with us during the time of the fight. You can tell us the secret now."

181

"Dad said that if he loses this fight, he will retire, and it will be the last one and that we will be enjoying a normal family life together. Why are you two crying?"

"We are just so happy, Arthur, mainly for your father."

"Mom, get the phone. Dad always calls us right after the fight."

"This is Dr. Edwards at the Hopkins Medical Center in New York City. I wanted to call you before you heard it on the news – your husband died from a brain hemorrhage that he suffered during his boxing match tonight. When he arrived in our emergency room it was too late for us to do anything to save him. I am so very sorry to have to be the one to tell you this bad news, and our condolences are with you and your family. I understand that his manager will be contacting you and will make all necessary arrangements to have your husband's body flown back to his hometown."

"Mom, please don't tell me it's bad news about Dad."

"Arthur, your father passed away. His brain was injured from the blows he took during the fight. We are going to have to be strong and live the life your father was working so hard to get for us. He left us financially secure with his life insurance and his money from the last fight, but he had to give up his life to realize his dream for us, which is just so sad. He will always be a champion in our home and in our hearts forever."

Horizon II

"We are here at Cape Canaveral, Florida to witness the lift off of the Horizon II spacecraft which is scheduled for a ten-day mission. Its stated goal is to place three satellites into orbit: one over California, one over Chicago, and one over New York City. These are for government use only. There are two other experiments that are listed as sensitive. We normally hear rumors about what the experiments are or watch what is loaded onto the spacecraft, but this time, we have not been able to pick up anything to explain these experiments. We will probably be able to find out what they were after the mission returns to Earth."

"This is mission control in Houston beginning the countdown for Horizon II. Five, four, three, two, one! We have lift off and all systems are go."

"We are pleased to announce that Horizon II has reached its orbit to conduct its mission with astronauts Mary Collins, Jay Johnston, and Dick Lovejoy on board. This mission is scheduled for ten days."

"Good job, crew of Horizon II. All satellites are in place and functioning beautifully. As you know, we still have two sensitive experiments to complete in the last three days of your mission. Contact Houston control if we can be of any assistance. Thank you. Houston control over and out."

. . .

"What the hell just happened? All our power has been lost. The computer system and navigation functions have been destroyed. Jay, contact Houston control and report our situation."

"All our communications channels are also destroyed. We are unable to contact Houston control. My guess is

183

that we went through an electrical magnetic field caused by a meteorite."

"Let's try to open all emergency channels and see if we can reach Houston."

"No such luck, Dick. We are dead in the water."

"Ask Mary if she has any ideas about how we can reach Houston. What did she say?"

"She said, 'Leave me the hell alone and don't eat all of the chocolate bars.'"

"Oh, that's right, she is experiencing her ladies' days to determine how this might affect women in space. She says she has only one more day to go."

"Okay, let's put on our space suits in order to cut down on the amount of oxygen we will be using. Keep the emergency channel open and hope for the best."

. . .

"Another day and no communications with Houston."

"Hi, guys. What are you up to?"

"Still trying to reach Houston control."

"How do you feel?"

"Completely back to normal."

"Have you tried Channel 2?"

"Yes, Mary. That was the first one we tried."

"My guess is that if I were Houston control, I would be working through Channel 2 as it is one that does not require an antenna. Let's try again."

"It means we will have to shut down all of our emergency channels first."

"Shut them down, Jay, it's worth a try."

"Okay, open Channel 2."

"Horizon II, this is Houston control. Do you read? Horizon II, this is Houston control. Do you read?"

"This is Horizon II, Houston control. Read you loud and clear."

"Wow, Mary, it's so good to hear your voice. Is everyone okay?"

"We are all fine, Houston, but nothing is working, as you already know."

"We will need your help in setting up the back computer system that has already been programmed with your reentry data. Once we have made sure it is up and working and has been programmed correctly, we will then reprogram the navigation backup system to get you into the correct orbit for reentry."

"We have tested the reentry rockets manually, and they are ready to be fired when you give us the word."

"Okay, good job, Horizon II. We will be giving you a four-hour notice when you will be in position to reenter your glide path."

"Horizon II, this is Houston control. All systems are up and running. You will notice that the spacecraft will be moving vertically to get you in the correct orbit. Be ready to reenter in about two hours."

"Is Mary there? I have a message from her mother."

"No, she is in the back of the spacecraft with Dick."

"Oh, okay, I'm sure it can wait. The experiment is more important."

. . .

"Dick, Houston says we have only two hours until reentry."

"This is not easy with this big helmet on. You should be able to pull your pants down without damaging the oxygen hose."

"How is Mary doing?"

"It's much easier for her."

"Okay, we need to be strapped in in one hour. So, get on with it."

"Houston control, this is Horizon II. We are all strapped in and ready for your command to reenter."

"Horizon II, you are now over your reentry position. The nose of the spacecraft should be in the up position."

"Okay, fire your reentry rockets now. You are on your glide path returning to Earth. Everything looks great from here."

. . .

"We are back at Cape Canaveral to watch the spacecraft Horizon II make its landing after a scare in which it lost communications with Houston control for several days. We even have the Vice-President here to greet the crew. We can see the spacecraft now as it approaches the landing strip. This crew will get a great big welcome from everyone here."

"The astronauts are being taken directly to an ambulance for transport to the medical center to be checked out and debriefed on this mission. We are now heading indoors for the NASA press conference."

"As all of you know, we had a harrowing experience with Horizon II when we lost all communications due to a meteorite passing within 500 miles of the spacecraft and creating an EMF that destroyed most of our electronics onboard. All's well that ends well. We will take a few questions."

"Were you able to perform the two sensitive experiments that were scheduled?"

"Yes, they were both completed to our utmost satisfaction."

"Can you now tell us what they were?"

"No, not at this time. That is all for now, and we want to thank you all for coming."

. . .

"We have been told that NASA will be holding a press conference today at 2 p.m., and it has something to do with the Horizon II mission. It has been three months since their return, so we can only surmise that it has something to do with the sensitive experiments that were performed in space."

"We want to thank you all for coming today to our press briefing, and we want to inform you that astronaut Mary Collins is three months pregnant, and the father is astronaut Dick Lovejoy. We picked this particular couple because they were already married when we began our planning to start a colony on Mars in the near future. This is, of course, the first child conceived in outer space."

"We would also like to ask your cooperation in refraining from sending us any more emails regarding a name for their son. Most of the names we've been receiving are centered around a space theme that could not possibly be used. One example is the name SPACEDICK, after his father. As you can see, this is not a good choice. That is all we have for this press briefing today. Thank you for coming. We'll keep you updated on any future developments as warranted."

Gala

"We are going to be the last ones to arrive at Foster's annual gala. It always seems that you have to stay late at the hospital on this date."

"Well, I got out as early as I could. At any rate, it's really good to see all of our friends in one place, not to mention spending an evening in a luxurious home on 35 acres of manicured grounds right here in Reidsville, Georgia."

"At least we will be arriving before the thunder and lightning storm arrives. It's supposed to be a really bad one."

. . .

"Good to see you, Charles. We've been looking forward to the annual Foster Gala."

"Attention everyone. Let me introduce Dr. Robert Webber and his wife Diane Webber to all of those who don't know them. Let me also introduce Gunter and Hilda Heinrich who are my lead engineers on our Panama construction project. They have never been to the United States before, so we are trying to show them as much of the United States as possible. We're really glad you could make it. We have the usual open bar, buffet, and band for dancing on the second floor. We'll probably be here until the early morning hours, so enjoy yourselves."

"Hello, Robert and Diane. We'd like to invite you to join us at our table."

"Thank you, Gunter."

"Let's go upstairs and dance a little before dinner."

"Robert doesn't dance."

"Oh, would he mind if I asked you to dance with me?"

"No, go right ahead. Diane is a really good dancer, as you will find out. Hilda and I will get along just fine."

. . .

"I think we'd better be getting back, Gunter."

"In Panama, it is very hard to find couples who are into swinging. In Europe it is a very common thing and easy to find couples. Any chance you and Robert would want to spend some time with me and Hilda?"

"I'm not into that, Gunther, and I'm sure Robert would never entertain such a thing."

"I'm sure Hilda is asking Robert the same, if he would be willing to spend time with her."

"Okay, let's go back downstairs. That's our table, right?"

"Yes, but where are Hilda and Robert?"

"Must have gone for a drink or something."

"Foster gave us our own room on the third floor. You don't suppose they could be up there, do you Diane? I'm going to go up and check to see if they are in the room. Care to join me?"

"No, even if they are in there, I'm not going to bed with you or anyone else."

"They will be down shortly. At least two people are enjoying the gala."

. . .

"Welcome back, you two. Diane and I have been having some great conversation while you were gone, but now I think we should try to meet some new people. Thanks for the dances, Diane."

"I am really surprised that you would do this right in front of me, Robert."

"I really had too much to drink, and I had no intention of spending time with Hilda, but after she got me to her room, things just got out of hand. I hope you can forgive me and let me make it up to you."

"Oh, great. We just lost the electricity. All the lights have gone out."

"Don't worry, we have a back-up generator which will turn on in very short order."

"Okay, we are back in business. That is quite some storm out there. It should pass through by 6 a.m. when we will be ending the gala."

"Where is Foster? I need to see him right away. Foster, there is a man lying outside on the lawn, and I think he's dead. You'd better call 911 right away."

"Show me where he is. Shit, it's Harry Willis, our pilot. What the hell could have happened? Why was he out in this type of weather?"

"Here are the ambulance and the police."

"Foster, do you know this man?"

"Yes, he is Harry Willis, our pilot."

"No one leaves these premises until they have been interviewed. This is now an active crime scene. Mr. Foster, please have all the people attending your gala placed in one room, and I will ask them all the same question so they can be on their way. Have any of you heard any noise or seen Harry Willis leave the premises?"

"No one heard or saw anything suspicious."

"Okay, you may all go, but we may want to contact you at a later date."

. . .

"Did you find anything in Harry Willis' room that might give us a clue as to why he was murdered?"

"Not a thing. No cell phone, no telephone numbers written down or anything else. Nothing was disturbed. He probably just walked outside to meet someone who had contacted him on his cell phone. That would be my best guess."

190

"We have no fingerprints, footprints, shell casings, cell phone or any other clues. This case is going cold before we have actually gotten started."

"Mr. Foster, you must have some idea why your pilot was murdered. Can you think back and try to remember anything that might give us a clue?"

"No, Detective, I cannot think of anything. If I do, I will contact you."

. . .

"It looks like the Harry Willis murder was an execution style murder."

"It has been three weeks, and we still don't have any suspects. We must be missing something. Let's go over what we have again."

. . .

"Hello, Diane. This is Roger. I thought I would call you after seeing you at the gala sitting there with Gunther and waiting for your husband to return with Hilda. You know, I've always had a crush on you and know that your husband leaves you alone most of the time, especially when he goes off to his conventions. If you ever want to spend some time with me, please give me a call. I am free anytime since I run my own business and can come and go as I please."

"Roger, you have been hitting on me for years now. Who knows, maybe I will call you, especially after what happened at the gala. Let me think about it."

. . .

"Let's go out to the airport and check with the maintenance people and see if anyone has been around the aircraft other than Mr. Foster and the new pilot. The plane is still in maintenance for the 5000-hour check. It will be finished in a few days."

191

"We don't know of anyone unusual who has been to see the aircraft. The only thing that was a little different was that one of the inspectors said there was a white residue in the rear cargo hold, and he thought it might be cocaine."

"Can we see the area you are talking about? Would you mind if we brought a sniffer dog to determine if it might actually be cocaine residue?"

"No problem."

"Well, guess what? This is our first real clue as to why Harry Willis was murdered. He either found out that the aircraft was being used to smuggle cocaine into the United States or he wanted a cut of the action."

"Let's contact Mr. Foster and find out when he will be flying off to Panama and when he will be returning. When the aircraft returns, we will have a video camera set up to film whoever removes the cocaine from the cargo hold and follow them to their place of operation."

. . .

"Diane, I'm going to Las Vegas for four days to a convention. Would you like to accompany me? It could be really fun."

"No, Robert, the last time I went with you, I wound up staying in the hotel room by myself. I think I'll pass this time."

. . .

"Okay, Roger, this is Diane. Robert is going out of town for four days, and I thought I would take you up on your offer to get together."

"This is a real surprise. I am free any time you want to meet."

"How about tomorrow about 1:00 at your house?"

"Sounds good. My house sets back from the road, so no one will see you when you arrive. See you then."

. . .

"Come on in, Diane. Welcome to my humble abode. I poured you a glass of wine. We can sit and talk for a while and get to know each other better."

"Aren't you going to have any wine, Roger?"

"No, but I'm going to enjoy a stick."

"What is a stick?"

"It's marijuana rolled up and soaked in a chemical that I think is cocaine, but I'm not really sure. I do know it gives a really great high."

"Where did you find those?"

"I was at a club in Atlanta, and I was offered them by this guy. I really liked them, and I bought ten to take home. Have you ever smoked a joint?"

"No, never."

"Would you like to try a few hits on this one?"

"Sure, why not. I'm over here with you committing adultery for the first time, I might as well try a stick for the first time."

"Draw it in and hold it and then exhale. Three times should be enough."

"Wow, this is making me feel like I'm flying. Whoa, whoa, this is great! I'm ready to move on whenever you are, Roger."

"Okay, let's enjoy ourselves. I never cook, so we are going to have to have something delivered."

"Pizza sounds fine to me. When are you going to light up another stick?"

"Why? Did you want to try it again? If you do, I will do it again."

"Okay, let's light up."

"Are you going to stay overnight?"

"If you want me to, I would like to stay."

"Someone's at the door. It must be the pizza delivery. I'll get it. Stay out of sight."

. . .

"Good morning. I was wondering if you feel like accompanying me to Atlanta tonight to go to the Aces Club where they really know how to party. It's also where Peter hangs out, and I need to buy more sticks. I'm down to two."

"I would need to go home and get showered and dressed for the trip. What time should I come back?"

"We will leave about 7:00."

"I really need to go into work today. Could I have one of your sticks to take with me while I'm getting ready?"

"Okay, looks like you really enjoy the high. See you at 7:00."

. . .

"I asked Mr. Foster, and he said he will be returning in two weeks for a board meeting on the 15th. He asked me why I wanted to know, and I told him we might have some new questions for him by then. He seemed okay with that answer. We are going to have to meet with the airport manager and advise him of what we are planning to do with the setting up of the video cameras as well as making certain that security is out of sight when the aircraft lands. Let's just hope that they have not been scared off and decide not to use this method again. If that is the case, we will never solve this murder."

. . .

"You are looking really great this evening, Diane. Things are just getting started here at Aces. Let's order our drinks and do some dancing while we wait for Peter to show up. He usually comes in late."

"Roger, I didn't expect to see you here tonight. Is this your date? You have done really well for yourself. She's beautiful. What can I do for you?"

"I need to buy some more sticks, about thirty, if you have them."

"Sorry, Roger, but you should have called first as the best I can do for you tonight would be ten. I can have thirty made and will call you when they're ready if that's okay."

"We were just about to leave, so we will meet you at our car. Here is your money. Give me a call when the thirty are ready."

"See you later."

. . .

"Seems like a longer drive back to Reidsville, but here we are in time to see the sun come up."

"Are you coming in and staying the rest of the day?"

"Yes, but I have to leave tonight since Robert will be coming home on Sunday morning. What are the chances that we can each take five of the sticks? I will give you the money tomorrow after I go to the bank."

"Are you sure you want to take five? I am starting to worry that you are enjoying smoking them too much."

"Don't worry, I will stretch them out."

. . .

"We just called Mr. Forster's office, and they stated his ETA is 4:00 p.m. Let's get everything in place. Here comes the plane taxiing up to the maintenance hangar. We may be here for a long time, so get some replacements, and we'll work twelve hour shifts."

. . .

"It has been two days, and no one has shown up to check the rear cargo hold. We could check it ourselves, but if we were spotted, it might tip off a maintenance employee and ruin everything."

"Let's just wait for one more day."

"Bill, this is Russ. We have two guys all dressed in black approaching the aircraft. They are opening the cargo hold. We can see an old tarp that they are unfolding, and it looks as though the suitcase was inside the tarp. They are walking away with the suitcase. They must have parked their auto near the entrance. We have two unmarked cars that will follow them to their operation site. They are pulling into a house on Beacon St., 151 Beacon. Have the video people set up in an area where they can catch anyone entering or leaving the facility."

"We found a great location to set up the video."

"Contact the District Attorney and see if we can get a search warrant to enter the house."

"The district attorney says that you will have to provide proof that you know that there were definitely drugs in the suitcase before a judge will sign a search warrant."

"Okay, we'll work on it."

. . .

"Robert, this is Roger. Diane went for it and spent two days and nights with me at my home. The videos are ready for you to pick up any time. I also have another great announcement. Your 40% interest in my company is going to pay off big-time. We just received a government contract. I'm working night and day to add a second shift and trying desperately to meet their demands. This contract is open-ended, and we have a mark-up of 50%."

"This sounds too good to be true."

"I don't think you have to worry about our ever having to use the videos in the divorce procedures. Diane will be too embarrassed to contest our offer – which will be a lot less than before we had the videos."

"Great, Hilda will be really happy to hear that. Thanks, again."

. . .

"Someone is driving up to the house now in a red Mercedes. He's getting out and walking into the house with a large backpack. This guy looks familiar. Oh, boy, it's Jeremy Foster, Mr. Foster's son who is attending Emory. There's the parking sticker on the rear window. He is coming out with the backpack and is getting into his car. We are going to follow him in our unmarked car and hope he makes some type of traffic violation. We have the radar on as well as the dash cam. We're approaching a 35 mile an hour zone, and he is still doing 50. Let's pull him over."

"We need to see your driver's license and registration. Do you know why we stopped you, Mr. Foster?"

"No."

"You were doing 50 in a 30 mile an hour zone. Can you get out of the car, please? Do you have any weapons or illegal drugs in your vehicle?"

"No."

"Do you mind if we look in your backpack?"

"Yes, I do."

"Is there something in there that you don't want us to find? We are going to have a sniffer dog check out your auto to see if you are telling us the truth about whether there are any drugs in your possession. You are really making it harder on yourself if you are lying to us."

"Okay, that was a hit. Let's open the backpack."

"Whoa, Mr. Foster. What are all these packets full of white powder? Could this be cocaine? We have a test kit in our car."

"Guess what, Mr. Foster? This is cocaine. Put him under arrest for possession of an illegal substance as well as a speeding ticket. Were you working for your father in Panama this summer before going off to college?"

"Yes."

. . .

"Roger, this is Diane. I haven't heard from you in over a week. What is going on?"

"I'm out of sticks. Are the thirty ready yet?"

"Things have changed. I was awarded a large government contract, and I have to work twelve hours a day, seven days a week to meet their demands. I have gone back to drinking beer and stopped the sticks. I need to keep my head in the game. I don't think you should smoke any more sticks either."

"Well, I'm going to drive down to Atlanta and pick up the thirty that Peter said he would have ready by now."

"I have already called Peter and told him that I was cancelling the order, so that won't do you any good."

"You bastard!"

. . .

"Call the District Attorney and see if he can now get a judge to sign off on a search warrant since we have proof that there is cocaine at that address."

"The District Attorney advises us that this will not be a problem. He suggests that you set up a swat team to go in early tomorrow morning about 5:00 when they should still be sleeping and make the arrests."

. . .

"Ready to crash through the door. Don't move! Stay where you are! Put the cuffs on them. Look at all this cocaine and the materials to weigh and package it for resale."

"Where is the gun?"

"Keep looking, it has to be here somewhere."

"Look what we just found in the bottom of the closet – a 22 caliber pistol. The same caliber that was used to murder Harry Willis. Now all we have to do is to make sure that the bullets taken from Harry Willis were fired from this gun, and we have our murderers. Great work, guys. CSI is on their way and will take all this in for evidence."

. . .

"Well, boys, guess what? This is the gun that was used to shoot Harry Willis. It appears that old Harry' wanted a piece of the action. They claim Jeremy Foster knew nothing about the operation. His only involvement was selling the coke at the university."

"I'm sure his dad will get him the best legal counsel possible."

"Let's go home for a few days and enjoy all our efforts in solving this case."

Release Date

"Do you have all your belongings, John?"

"I have just what I came in with twenty years ago."

"You must have really pissed off the U.S. government. As I notice on your release papers, they stopped every parole hearing that was scheduled for you. It is rare these days that a person who did not commit a violent act has to serve his entire sentence. Do you have someone to meet you at the gate and give you a ride?"

"Yes, my sister Sandy will be picking me up."

"Okay, John, good luck, and don't come back, okay?"

. . .

"Hey, Sandy!"

"It's so good to see my big brother finally out of jail. Get in the car, and let's get you back to my house. We've made a small apartment for you in our basement that I think you'll like. No one knows that you are coming to live with us. Someone is approaching our car. Yes, sir, may I help you?"

"Yes, I'm FBI Agent Sam Frank, and I just want John to know that I will be watching his every move. This missing gold shipment is still the property of the U.S. government, and we want it back. Thank you for your time."

"The FBI still believes that you are the one who knows where the gold is hidden, and they won't give up until they are sure you don't know where it is. Let's get out of here and head back to Homestead. I never want to see the Florida State Prison again."

. . .

"It's been three months, John, since your release, and now you even know how to use a cell phone and iPad. You seem to be getting used to being on the outside very well after all those years. I'm proud of you, John. Hey, I'm going to need your help. One of my cats died, and I want to bury it in the woods. Could you do that for me?"

"Sure, Sandy, no problem. Drop me off at the hardware store, and I will purchase a shovel, and we'll drive to the woods outside of town so I can bury it for you."

"This looks like a good place, John. Let's stop here. The cat is in a bag in the trunk. I think this is a perfect spot for the burial. Make sure you go back in far enough that no one will find it."

"Okay, Sandy. Wait here."

"Hello, Michelle. I'm just sitting here in the woods waiting for John to come back from burying my cat. What the heck? There is a helicopter overhead and four black sedans pulling up, and they are going into the woods with their guns drawn. I can hear the loudspeaker from the helicopter telling John to get on the ground and put his hands on his head. I'm going to leave before they start questioning me. John will have to get his own ride back to town. I'm going to have to hang up now, Michelle. Call you later."

. . .

"Rick, there is a report that the FBI has someone trapped in the woods off Route 4 using a helicopter and a bunch of agents. We have to get over there fast and find out what's going on. I'm so excited. This will be our first real investigation for the Beacon Times as crime reporters."

"Okay, Fred, we're on our way. It looks like the FBI agents are leaving, and the helicopter is also gone.

201

What's going on here? Here comes someone walking out of the woods. Were you the person that the FBI was following into the woods?"

"Looks like that to me. They were looking for an escaped convict, and I guess they thought I look a lot like him. Could you guys give me a lift into town? I would really appreciate it. My name is John."

"I'm Rick Mutter, and this is Fred Witt. We are investigative reporters for the Beacon Times."

"You guys must be just out of college. You look awfully young to be doing this kind of work without a seasoned person to mentor you. If you could drop me off at the McDonald's on Broadway, I would greatly appreciate it. Thanks for the ride, guys."

"Sandy, I'm at the McDonald's on Broadway. Can you pick me up? You will be able to recognize me as I will be the guy standing out front with a shovel."

"Very funny, John. I'll be there in a few minutes. The FBI wasn't kidding when they said they were watching your every move. They must have been very upset when they found out you were just burying a dead cat."

. . .

"Rick, I know we are new at this, but something tells me that the FBI, and not the local police, were involved in this operation. We should have asked John for his last name. We not only don't know his last name, but also we don't know where he lives. But, we could still write a good story with what we know now. Let's start there for this week's edition."

. . .

"Sandy, do you remember that old building that I was renting where I used to work on restoring the 1929 Packard that Uncle Mike gave to me?"

"Sure, I drove by there a couple of months ago, and it was in awful shape. It looked like it was about to fall down."

"Could you drive me there? I want to check to see if anything of mine might still be there."

"Sure, John, let's go."

"Wait here, and I'll be right back. You were right about the condition."

. . .

"Frank, this is Tim. We are watching John Herlund going into an old building. I have him in my range using the binoculars. Stay on the line, and I will let you know when he comes out. Wait, there he is. He has a large, old metal box. I can see an old Pan American logo on the top of the box. He's heading for the car that is waiting for him. What do I do now?"

"Move in and arrest him. Take the box and put it in your trunk."

"What are the charges for the arrest?"

"Trespassing and looting. Cuff him and read him his rights. Bring him into Miami-Dade for booking and processing. Have him put into a holding cell until we can bring him before a judge on Monday morning."

"Okay, will do."

"This is Agent Frank from the Miami office. We have just arrested John Herlund with a large, old metal box that we believe contains the missing gold. How do you want us to handle this? We need instructions from Washington."

"We have decided to send a private jet to pick up the box. Drive it to Opa Locka Airport and load it onto the plane. Set up a three van caravan with the gold being in the middle van and drive it to Opa Locka. We'll be arriving at 10:00 p.m. tonight. The box will be taken directly to our crime lab in Quantico for processing. An

Assistant Deputy Director will also be on hand from headquarters."

. . .

"Okay, let's open the box. Make certain all of this is on video. Okay, let's have a look. Oh, shit, guys. No gold in this box, only old tools probably belonging to John Herlund. I would suggest returning them to him right away, and also, apologize for the mistake we made. I have a feeling this is not going to end well."

. . .

"John, your attorney, Robert Silverman, is here to bail you out. He said your sister hired him. She knows how to pick a good attorney as he is one of the best defense attorneys in Miami. Hold on, I have to take this phone call. I've been informed that we've dropped all charges and owe you an apology for what we put you through. There is no need for a bail bondsman, Attorney Silverman. We've dropped all charges and apologized to John for the mix up."

"Okay, fine."

"I'll drive you home, John."

"Let's get out of here."

"Your sister filled me in on all the details of your arrest, and I can assure you that if you want me to file a lawsuit in Federal Court against the Federal Government for false arrest, false imprisonment, and violation of your civil rights under the U.S. Constitution, I can. We will also ask for 25 million in damages. Believe me, we have a great case here."

"Okay, go ahead with the suit. It would be a great feeling to beat the FBI after what they put me through for the last twenty years."

. . .

"Rick, this is your buddy Doug with the Miami Examiner. How are things going at the Beacon Times?"

"Great, Doug. What's up?"

"We just were told that a federal lawsuit was filed here in Miami against the FBI on behalf of John Herlund, and he is listed as living in Homestead, which is right in your backyard. Thought you might want to check it out once you google his name. Keep me posted if anything develops. We should get together for a drink sometime."

"Thanks, Doug. We are on it."

"Fred, google John Herlund and see what comes up."

"Wow, you won't believe this. Here is his picture. Look familiar?"

"Shit, that's the guy we gave a ride to McDonald's."

"He was just released from Florida State Prison three months ago and completed a twenty-year sentence after being convicted of stealing a shipment of gold from the Pan American Airways cargo warehouse. The gold was never found. That explains why they were chasing him in the woods. They thought he was going to dig up the gold. His story about the FBI looking for an escaped convict was a lie."

"We need to get his home address and see if we can get an interview with him. Call your friend at the police department and have them run a DMV check to see if we can get an address where he is staying."

"Hello, Jack. This is Rick Mutter at the Beacon Times. I need to ask you a favor. Can you run a name for me through DMV? I need an address."

"Sure, what is the name?"

"John Herlund."

"Okay, hold on. Nothing comes up under that name, and I have checked registration also – nothing. Sorry guys."

"The only people we know that have his address are the FBI, and we sure as hell won't be getting it from them.

Let's call it a night and try to come up with a way to get what we need."

. . .

"Good morning, Rick. Get in the car because we're driving to the Florida State Prison to try to find out who picked up John when he was released. He is, most likely, staying with that person."

"Great idea, but who at the prison is going to give up that information?"

"I don't know yet, but it's worth a try. Here we are. It looks like we have to stop at the guard shack. Good morning, sir. We are reporters from the Beacon Times, and we need to find out who picked up a person that was discharged three months ago. Can you steer us in the right direction?"

"Do you know the date of discharge?"

"Yes, sir, it was July 14. The name is John Herlund."

"Let me check our log. He was picked up by his sister, Sandra Anderson. The only address is Homestead, Florida."

"Thanks a million. That's a great help."

"Fred, start searching Sandra Anderson on your phone, and let's see what we come up with. Start with all of the social media sites, first."

"No luck. She's not listed on any sites. Wait a minute, her name did come up in the obituary column of the Miami Herald, which is dated fifteen years ago. It reads that a Captain David Anderson, U.S. Army Reserve, was killed in Iraq. He leaves behind a wife, Sandra Anderson, and two children. The address listed is 56 Dodge St., Homestead, Florida. He will be buried in the Arlington National Cemetery in Arlington, Virginia. Let's hope that she is still at that address. If not, we will have to run her through the DMV."

"You know, Rick, we have a natural ability to find the facts that are below the surface that others don't see.

206

The next generation of journalists will not be looking to Woodward and Bernstein but to Mutter and Witt as their role models in investigative journalism."

"Or it could be Witt and Mutter."

"Okay, let's knock on the door and see who answers. Are you Sandra Anderson?"

"Yes, I am. What can I do for you boys?"

"We are looking to interview John Herlund. We gave him a ride back to McDonald's with his shovel. I am Rick Mutter, and this is Fred Witt. We are journalists with the Beacon Times."

"We have enjoyed reading your last two articles although they were somewhat vague. Just teasing. I'll check with John to see if he will agree to an interview."

"Come on in, guys. Make yourselves at home. What are you here for, exactly?"

"We now know that you lied to us about the FBI looking for an escaped convict, that you have filed a suit against the U.S. government, and that the FBI is still looking for the missing gold from the Miami gold heist. We know that you have always professed your innocence. We are interested in knowing if there is anything that you want to tell us that you might want the public to know in our next story."

"There is one thing I would like you to write on my behalf, and that is to explain how, after serving a full twenty-year sentence, the FBI is still making my life miserable. I can't go anywhere or do anything without them following me. I can't even make a phone call because my phones are tapped. If you could write a story that would get the public to think I have been prosecuted enough, that would be great. If you don't know, I was arrested and jailed just one month ago, which is why I filed the lawsuit. The FBI finally dropped all charges and released me and admitted they had made a grave mistake. Put that in your story, and I will be forever grateful to you."

"We will, John, and I think you'll enjoy the way we frame the story. Thanks again for the interview, and good luck with the lawsuit."

. . .

"My name is Sandra Anderson, and this is my attorney Joshua Weiss. We would like to talk to Agent Frank if at all possible. I'm the sister of John Herlund."

"Come right this way. I will escort you to Agent Frank's office."

"Good morning. I'm Sandra Anderson, and this is my attorney Joshua Weiss."

"We are very familiar with Mr. Weiss, and I think we spoke when you were picking up John on the day of his release. So, what brings you here today?"

"I have a proposition for you regarding the missing gold from the Miami gold heist that my brother was convicted of. I would like to make two statements before we start with our demands. One, I do not know, at this time, where the gold is, and two, I will not communicate with you again. All future communications, if there are any, will be done through Mr. Weiss. Is that understood?"

"No problem. This would not be the first negotiation we have had with Mr. Weiss."

"Our demands are that I receive the 20 million reward for the missing gold offered by the FBI – tax free. John will receive, also tax free, the 25 million for the lawsuit settlement, plus attorney fees. Also, John and I both want an immunity agreement for any charges now or in the future pertaining to this case."

"As you are aware, this decision would have to be made at the highest levels of the Bureau and not at my level. I will present it to Washington as soon as Mr. Weiss delivers the official proposal to this office. I will then convey our decision to him for further action, if any needs to be taken. Again, thanks for coming in, and I will escort you out."

. . .

"Sandra, this is Joshua Weiss. Good news, the FBI has just delivered two checks totaling 45 million and two immunity agreements signed, sealed, and delivered. I must admit, I didn't really believe this would happen, but it is all set. All we need now is to give me the location of the gold, and once it is in their possession, I am authorized to give you the money. Do you have the location site that I am supposed to give the FBI?"

"Yes, I do. The gold is buried behind the McDonald's on Broadway in the wooded area. There are two large trees that are separated by only six feet. The gold is buried between those two trees. Have them call you when they have the gold in their possession so we know for sure there have been no slipups."

"I promise to call you immediately, and you can come by and pick up your money and deposit it that very day."

. . .

"Fred, there is a phone call for you on Line 3. It's a man, but he would not identify himself."

"Fred Witt here. How can I help you?"

"I am going to help you, Fred. You are going to get the biggest scoop of your career. Listen closely. Go to the McDonald's on Broadway with a video camera. Make sure you are not seen. You will see FBI agents coming out of the woods behind McDonald's carrying the missing gold shipment from the Miami heist. Take a few still photos for your paper and the video for your website. The FBI will be putting pressure on you after you publish your findings. Don't take a polygraph test. Stick to saying that an anonymous caller was how you found out. Stick with it. Don't waver one bit. Get there early in the morning or you will miss it. Good luck. Now, you are going to be rich and famous."

. . .

"Sandra, this is Joshua Weiss. The FBI just called to say that they have the gold in their possession, but they are really pissed off and want to know who tipped off the journalists at the Beacon Times and had them video their operation."

"You can tell them it certainly wasn't me or John. I bet the tip came from inside the Bureau. Tell them to polygraph all of their people and find out who did this. That will really piss them off even more. John and I are leaving the country for an extended vacation and want to thank you for all your work on our behalf. After that, you should contact the guys at the Beacon Times since they are now going to be in need of a good lawyer to handle their affairs."

Rage

"Mark, answer your phone."

"Right. Good morning. Mark here."

"Hello, Mark. I hate to disturb you on a Sunday, but we have a double homicide at the Crestview Apartments in Brooklyn. The CSI team is already on route to the scene, and the police have roped it off. I don't have any other homicide detectives that can help you with this investigation. You are all alone on this one. Sorry about that. Good luck."

"Thanks a lot, Jack. I'm on my way."

. . .

"Hello, Detective Mark Walsh, so this is your assignment?"

"I'm afraid so, Sergeant. What can you tell me about this so far?"

"Two victims, one a female and one a male, both stabbed repeatedly. Both were pronounced dead when we arrived, and it looks like they were murdered several days ago. The CSI team is already inside doing their thing."

"Okay, thanks. Hi, guys. What have you found so far?"

"Nothing that we can use as evidence so far, no fingerprints, no murder weapon, and no DNA that we can find. There was no evidence of a forced break in, so apparently, the victims let the killers in. This is about as brutal a murder scene as I have ever witnessed. There is no evidence that anything is missing, so robbery was not the motive. From the identification, we have found that the female was Tia Gomez, and the male was Elvin Jones. We have their cell phones and will get back to you if we find anything that might point you in the way of a suspect. This is going to be a tough one, Mark. Do you have any other homicide detectives helping you on this case?"

"No, we are really shorthanded right now."

"I interviewed the tenants who are directly above and below this apartment, as well as the tenants on both sides, to see if they saw or heard anything. Of the three tenants I interviewed, no one heard or saw anything suspicious. There was one apartment, which was right next door to the murdered victims' apartment, where the tenants were not home. I will make a note to go back or call them later."

"Mark, we have located Tia Gomez's place of employment from her cell phone. The only other calls were to her boyfriend, so no help there. She was employed at Alton Plastic Works in Brooklyn."

"Thanks, I'll check with them tomorrow when they open for business."

. . .

"Good morning, gentlemen. I am Detective Mark Walsh from the homicide division investigating the death of Tia Gomez. She was found murdered yesterday in her boyfriend's apartment. I would appreciate your letting me talk to her closest friends to see if they might have information that might help in solving this case."

"I think you will want to talk to Maria Irving. Those two were always hanging out together. She really didn't have any other close friends here that I know of. I will have Maria meet you in my office so you can have some privacy."

"Okay, thanks. Hello, Maria. I am Detective Mark Walsh, and I'm afraid I have some bad news to report. Your friend Tia Gomez was found murdered in her boyfriend's apartment yesterday. I know this is really a shock to you, but I really need you to answer some questions for me. Can you do that?"

"Yes, what is it you want to know?"

"Do you know of anyone who would want to harm Tia?"

"The only person upset with Tia was Bernie who works with us. Tia always turned him down when he made advances and was always upset whenever she had a new boyfriend."

"What did she tell you about Elvin Jones?"

"She met him about three weeks ago and thought he was a really nice guy. That's all I really know."

"Do you know the home address of Tia's parents and their telephone number?"

"Yes, I will get them for you."

"Thank you for all your help, Maria. Can you ask your boss to send in Bernie? I would like to ask him a few questions. Thank you. Bernie, I'm Detective Mark Walsh from the homicide division of the Brooklyn Police Department investigating the death of Tia Gomez. I understand you had a real thing for her, but she would never entertain any of your advances, which really upset you. Is this right?"

"I might have been a little pissed off, but I surely didn't kill her."

"Where were you this weekend?"

"I was in Connecticut visiting my parents who were celebrating their 50th anniversary. My brothers and sisters were also there. I left Friday afternoon and came back Sunday night. Here is my parents' phone number. Call them, and they will verify my staying with them all weekend."

"Okay, thanks, Bernie. I will check it out."

"This is Mark Walsh. Did the autopsy report come in yet?"

"Good timing, Mark, just received it. This was not a sexual attack. The report also indicates that there must have been more than one attacker, which makes this case even more complex."

"It just doesn't make sense that a jealous lover would have help in committing the murder."

"If it wasn't a sexual attack and wasn't a robbery, what was the reason?"

"We have been checking the background of Elvin Jones and can find no record of his being in trouble before. We don't believe it was drug related, either, which makes this one a tough puzzle for you, Mark. We do have the workplace address of Elvin Jones. He worked for Mike's Car Rental in Brooklyn. It's a very small company. We also have his parents' phone number and address for you. We will let you know if we come up with anything else, Mark. Good luck."

. . .

"Good morning, guys. I'm Detective Mark Walsh from the homicide division of the Brooklyn Police Department investigating the murder of Elvin Jones. I understand he worked for you. Is that right?"

"Yes, sir."

"What can you tell me about Mr. Jones that might help me in solving this case?"

"Elvin was a great employee. He was always on time, and the customers loved him. There are only six of us, and we all got along great."

"Would you say Mr. Jones was a drug user?"

"To be honest, he never used any drugs while on the job, but he did mention he used cocaine for recreation on the weekends. That's all we really know about his personal life, other than the fact that he had recently met a girl that he really liked."

"Okay, guys, thanks for your help."

. . .

"Good morning, Mr. and Mrs. Jones. I'm Detective Mark Walsh investigating the death of your son. I know this is a difficult time for you, but I really need to ask you some questions, if that's okay."

"Sure, Detective. What are the questions?"

"Do you know if your son was ever involved in using or selling drugs?"

"We actually didn't see him that much lately as he had a new girlfriend that he seemed to be really infatuated with. We never had a problem with Elvin using drugs, and I don't think he was involved in selling them. The only thing I heard was when he was talking to someone on his cell phone and said he was thinking of joining the Black Knights Club. This was a bad sign to me, as we all know who the Black Knights are. I don't know whether he actually followed up or not. He had no known enemies who would want to kill him. I won't rest until you guys find out what was the real reason for his murder."

"We will let you know right away, as soon as we are absolutely sure. Thank you for your help."

"This is Mark Walsh checking in. I just left the Jones residence and am heading over to the Black Knights' gang headquarters as Elvin's father thought he might be a member of that gang. I will be at the office after talking to them."

. . .

"Who wants in?"

"Detective Mark Walsh. I want to talk to you about one of your members."

"Okay, Mark, but keep your badge where we can see it when you enter."

"Who is in charge that I could talk to?"

"That would be me, Big Ed."

"Okay, Big Ed, I want to show you a picture of a person who was murdered Sunday. We were led to believe that he was a member of your gang. Here is the picture. Do you recognize him? His name is Elvin Jones."

"Never seen this man in my life. Definitely not a member of our club, Mark."

"Are you sure?"

"Look, don't piss me off any more than I already am."

"Okay, I have a picture of a girl who was murdered along with Elvin. Do you recognize her?"

"Hell, no, I don't recognize her. I'm sure you're here because you think this was some kind of a drug related killing, but I can assure you that we have never been accused of harming a woman. That is something we would never do. Check with your people who track the gangs in Brooklyn, and they will tell you that. That's all I have for you, Mark. Let me see you to the door before I lose my temper and tell you what I really think about the corrupt Brooklyn Police Department. Have a nice day."

"This is Mark Walsh. Can you patch me in to the division that tracks the gangs in Brooklyn? Okay, thanks."

"Phil Murphy here. What's up?"

"Mark Walsh from homicide. I just left the Black Knights and was told by Big Ed that they would never harm a woman and that you could verify this was true. I'm investigating two murder victims, one being a young woman."

"You got to interview Big Ed? Congratulations. We haven't been able to do that for some time. Funny you should call now because we're about to make a big bust on a shipment of drugs coming into the Black Knights' possession. Keep reading the newspapers. Speaking of reading the newspapers, it sounds like you have more of a rage killing than a drug dispute. But, who knows for sure? Anything else, Mark?"

"No, that's all for now. Thanks again."

216

"Hey, look who just walked into the office. Where have you been, Mark, on vacation?"

"Don't be a wise-ass, Tom."

"Have you made any progress on the double homicide victims?"

"No, not yet. None of my leads have panned out so far. I'm going home to get some sleep and will get a fresh start in the morning."

"Did you want me to tell the Chief anything?"

"Nothing to report, Tom."

"Okay, see you tomorrow."

. . .

"Good morning. This is Detective Walsh. I'm just checking in to let you know that I'm going back to Crestview Apartments to interview Mr. Wilkerson who is the apartment manager. After that, I will return to the office."

. . .

"Good morning, Mr. Wilkerson. I want to sit down with you and go over any and all details that you might remember about Elvin Jones and also his neighbors. Let's start with Elvin. Were there any problems with him as a tenant?"

"We did have one major complaint, and that was he played his music too loudly. I finally told him that I would have to start eviction proceedings if he didn't stop. He informed me that he had lost most of his hearing from taking too much OxyContin and had to go into rehab to get off of it. He wasn't aware of how loud it really was. I informed him that he had to buy a headset and listen to his music that way or he was out of here. To make matters worse, he worked until ten o'clock and came

217

home late, just when everyone else was going to bed. He also admitted he used cocaine and sometimes would forget what time it was, but that it would not happen again. That was just two days before he was murdered."

"I already talked to three of the tenants except the one who wasn't home. Is there anything else you can remember?"

"No, that was the only problem we had with Elvin Jones."

"Okay, Mr. Wilkerson. Thanks again."

. . .

"Any luck with Mr. Wilkerson, Mark?"

"I really don't know yet until we run all these names through for background checks. I might have been looking in all the wrong places. The answer might have been right under my nose."

"Mark, we ran the names through our computer files, and you are going to be surprised what tenants are in Apartment 414 which shares a common wall with 415, Elvin Jones' apartment. The occupants are Joe Mitchell and Larry Albright. Here are their rap sheets. Look at their arrests for violent crimes and the manufacturing and distributing of meth. They are also heavy users. Apparently, neither one is employed, and we called Mr. Wilkerson, and he said they always paid their rent on time and in cash. You might want to take a closer look at these two guys. They were both released from prison almost one year ago."

"Chief, we have two possible suspects in our homicide investigation. Would you send two squad cars to their apartment and request that they come in for questioning? I realize that they can refuse, and we will have no recourse to make them comply. Let's just see how it goes."

"Okay, Mark. Let's hope we are on to something here."

"Mark, this is Sergeant Stanford. We have both individuals and are on our way back to the station."

"Okay, great. When you get here, place one of them in Interview Room 3 and the other in 5, and let me know when that is completed. Good work, Sergeant."

"Chief, they are on their way in, and we will be interviewing them in separate rooms. We'll keep you advised if we have anything concrete."

"Thanks, Mark."

"Tom, both suspects are coming in. I will interview one, and I want you to interview the other; we'll compare before they are released."

"Okay, Mark, will do."

"Good afternoon. I'm Detective Mark Walsh investigating the murder that took place in the apartment next to yours. I understand Elvin Jones was a real asshole when it came to playing his music out loud and disturbing other tenants. Tell me about it."

"We spoke to him many times, but he still insisted on pissing everybody off and didn't seem to care, but now we won't have that problem to worry about anymore."

"I need you to take off your shoes for me. Will you do that, please?"

"Okay, but do I get them back?"

"Sure, no problem. I'll be back in a second. Take these sneakers down to the lab to see if there is any blood on them. I noticed some dark spots on the side. Tell them to put a rush on it and that you will wait for the results. They have the DNA of both Elvin and Elizabeth to compare them with if they find anything. Thanks, I will make sure to keep him here until we get the results. Tom, can you come out here for a moment? See if you can get your man to take off his shoes and send them to the lab. Keep him talking until we get the results back."

"Let me get the door, Joe. Here are your lab results, Mark."

"Bingo."

"You're kidding."

"No, on the soles of the sneakers were blood traces from both Elizabeth and Elvin."

"Great job."

"Well, Joe, it looks like you won't be getting your sneakers back after all. We are going to use them as evidence to send you to death row. Both victims' blood was found on the bottom of your sneakers. I will read you your rights and advise you that we are charging you with two counts of first degree murder. Cuff him, Sergeant, and take him down to booking."

"Mark, we have the lab results for Larry Albright, and they were completely clean."

"Okay, tell Tom to stop the interview and come out here. Tom, we found enough evidence on Joe Mitchell to charge him but not Larry. I want you to book Larry on suspicion of conspiracy in helping Joe commit the murder. We can hold him at least 24 hours, which will give me time to get a search warrant signed for their apartment."

"Okay, will do, Mark. Great news. Wow."

"Chief, we are getting a warrant signed now to search the apartment of our two suspects and, hopefully, we will find additional evidence. We'll keep you informed. I know the press has been all over this, but we should have enough for you to give a press conference soon."

"Mark, I'm sending two of our CSI team with you to check for things you might overlook."

"Okay, Chief, great."

"So far, Mark, we have found a meth lab with all of the necessary chemicals as well as 15K in cash."

"Business must have been pretty good."

"We are still looking for the murder weapon, but no luck so far."

"Look at what we just found, a garbage bag which not only contains the murder weapon but two sets of bloody clothing, one for each killer. This should be enough to also connect Larry to the crime."

"Good work, Mark. We can wrap this up with that additional evidence."

"What happened here was that these two guys were really high on meth, and when Elvin started to play his music, they became extremely violent, which is what happens when meth takes over. Most killers on meth claim they don't remember anything about the crime. These guys were completely out of their minds when they killed those two people."

"This won't be the last time we see a violent crime caused by meth."

"A crime like this really makes me worry about what the future holds, especially for our own kids."

"I know what you mean. Take some time off with your wife and kids."

"You don't have to tell me twice. I'm out of here."

Jealousy

I watched as she entered the door of the restaurant, and I thought she was one of the most beautiful women I had ever seen – long, wavy blonde hair, green eyes and an incredible body. Then, I saw it for the first time. As she turned around to take her seat, there was this large pink and blue scar from the top of her forehead, over her eye, and down her cheek to the bottom of her jawline. Something came over me at that moment that I can't explain. I couldn't take my eyes off her and hoped she wouldn't notice me staring at her.

I left the restaurant after hurriedly paying the cashier so that I could make the morning meeting at the drug enforcement office. Today, it included input from the Bogota Chief of Police, the Attorney General's Office, and Columbian Homeland Security. After the meeting, I asked the Chief of Police if he knew anything about a striking woman with a dramatic scar over her face. He said that her name was Dolores Andreas and that she had been driven to the hospital in Bogota by ambulance from a small town named La Quinta. The Chief had sent a policewoman to visit her in the hospital to see if law enforcement could be of any assistance, but she insisted she didn't need any help. She claimed not to know her attacker in La Quinta. Naturally, my first thought was that she was involved with a cruel boyfriend, a controlling husband or maybe even a dangerous drug dealer.

I didn't see her for about a week, and then one morning, she came into the restaurant, and I resolved to follow her. I wanted to find out where she lived, but she got into a cab and disappeared into the city traffic. Thinking that it would be worthwhile to drive to La Quinta to see what I could find out about her and the mysterious scar, I spotted a busy restaurant that seemed to be full of locals. When the waitress served my lunch, I asked her if she knew Dolores Andreas. She said she did not but politely offered to check with other employees to see if they knew of her. She came back with my check with disappointing news. Even the older woman cashier who had been there for years had never heard of her.

Disappointed, I left the restaurant only to find that all four of my tires had been slashed. I wondered if I had been recognized as DEA but had no time to figure that out. I called the closest garage for a tow and pumped the mechanic for information on Dolores. The minute I mentioned her name, he suggested that I gas up the car, lock my doors, and leave La Quinta without delay. "You stand out. You look like a government agent, which may be your problem," he said shoving me out the door.

As I was leaving La Quinta, I heard a siren and looked in my rearview mirror. I saw the red, blue, and yellow blinking lights and pulled over. A young policeman asked me for my driver's license and registration. I handed it over promptly and waited for him to explain himself. He called me by name, Daniel Edwards, and asked if I had had a nice visit in La Quinta. I told him I did. "Do you have any intention of returning anytime soon?" he asked looking me directly in the eye. I told him I would be leaving for the United States later in the week and that I would not be back. He returned my license and registration and told me I "should have" a "nice, safe trip back to Bogota." His words seemed more like a final command than good wishes for a pleasant journey.

The following day, after arriving back in Bogota, I realized I should have asked if there was another Andreas in La Quinta; however, none were listed when I called information. I decided to call the garage where my car had been repaired to try to find out if Dolores had any relatives living in La Quinta. The manager answered the phone. He was reluctant to give me an address, but he did tell me that Dolores had been raised by her grandmother, Mrs. Ava Santiago and then abruptly hung up the phone.

I called information and was able to get a listing for Mrs. Santiago. After all that I had done to get to this moment, I was surprisingly nervous about making the call. Would my interest in Dolores come across as odd? After all, I was a stranger to both women. However, I felt compelled to finish what I had started, so I made the call.

Mrs. Santiago answered the phone. She was quite pleasant and willing to hear me out. I told her I was someone who wanted to help her granddaughter, that I would like to visit so that I could explain how. Mrs. Santiago seemed to sense that I meant no harm, and once she realized that her granddaughter was not in any trouble, she was curious enough to invite me to meet her. I explained that it would be better for both of us if I arrived late in the evening so as not to attract any attention. Mrs. Santiago described her home as being on the outskirts of La Quinta which made it that much safer for me. I told her I would be there on Saturday around 8 o'clock.

I arrived at Mrs. Santiago's comfortable home, and she was most gracious, offering me drinks and food that I declined. I told her I knew that what I wanted to discuss was a painful subject to talk about but that I really wanted to know what had happened to Dolores. She started by showing me pictures of Dolores as she was growing up. She told me how Dolores had always been the most beautiful girl in town. All of the boys and men had lusted after her, but Mrs. Santiago assured me that Dolores never had anything to do with anyone in La Quinta. She had been dedicated, heart and soul, to teaching English at the local high school and had moved into her own apartment.

Life had been happy for Dolores until the day the rumors started. Certain young men bragged that they

224

had been to her apartment and had stayed overnight. Mrs. Santiago had received a threatening phone call from a woman who screamed that Dolores had better stop sleeping with the married men. Mrs. Santiago had assured the woman that these stories were untrue, but she refused to listen and hung up.

One week later, Dolores received a knock at her door late at night, and when she opened it, the offended wives rushed in. "And you know what happened," said Dolores' grandmother with her steely eyes focused on the past as she thought about that horrible night. "Dolores really can't remember anything about what happened next. She was rushed to Bogota by ambulance and hasn't been back to La Quinta since, not even to see me. But she has not forgotten us. She calls me at least once a week."

I took a deep breath and made my proposal. "I would like you to give her a message, please. Tell her that you met with me, and I would like to take her, at my expense, to see a plastic surgeon to remove her scar." Mrs. Santiago was quiet for a few minutes, but she accepted the card with my phone number on it and agreed to speak with her granddaughter for me.

. . .

"Hello, Mr. Edwards? This is Dolores Andreas. I received a phone call from my grandmother who said you had paid her a visit and were asking her questions about me. Why would you go to such lengths to find out this information?"

"Well, as your grandmother told you, I saw you at the restaurant where I went for breakfast. Perhaps we could meet there, and I could explain in person what I am trying to accomplish. Would you be open to that?"

"Yes, I suppose so because my grandmother would be very disappointed if I didn't."

225

"Fair enough. Let's meet at the restaurant at 8:00 tomorrow morning."

"Since I don't know what you look like, please join me at my table. Goodbye, Mr. Edwards."

"Goodbye, Dolores."

. . .

"Good morning, Dolores. I'm Dan Edwards. It's a pleasure to meet you. Your grandmother is such an elegant and kind woman."

"Yes, we are very close. So, what brings you to Columbia, Mr. Edwards?"

"Please call me Dan. I'm in Bogota because I work for the U.S. government. I hope that doesn't scare you away."

"No, not at all. Why should it?"

"I'm glad of that. I am part of a team that is advising Columbian law enforcement in the use of new surveillance equipment such as drones and other means of locating cocaine manufacturing facilities and transport."

"This will come as a surprise to you, but there is a connection between our jobs. I work for a local bank in charge of new accounts. Many of the deposits I handle are from people who, most likely, have earned this money in illegal activities. Because of the four languages I speak, I am able to set up accounts in foreign banks for our clients. You might not want to associate with someone involved in this line of work."

"If you are saying that you are laundering money from the drug cartels, I have news for you. Every local bank in Columbia is doing the same, maybe not to such a great extent, but they are involved. The Columbian government does not seem to want to interfere because this money was earned after the drugs were out of the country. In many ways, the cartel money helps maintain the Columbian economy, which is why I don't think we

226

have anything to worry about. But, please, let me explain my interest in you."

"My grandmother already mentioned something about it. Dan, if you came here because you feel sorry for me and think you can change my life, I must tell you that you are wasting your time. I love my life, and I have come to accept my fate and this scar as my cross to bear. I can do so without any sense of inferiority or any feeling that my beauty has suffered as a result of it."

"It is hard for me to explain my feelings for you, and it would not matter to me whether or not you have the scar removed."

"Are you saying that this is about caring for me? You do not even know me."

"I guess I'm asking you for a date to see where this caring might lead us. Is that a possibility?"

"How can I not feel flattered by your interest? My grandmother thinks you are the answer to her prayers for me."

"Then, I will take your smile as a yes."

"There is only one problem, if my employers were to find out that you are a government agent, I would be in a difficult position. We should both think carefully about meeting again."

"That is a reasonable concern. Let's leave it at this; if you return for breakfast tomorrow, I will be waiting for you."

"I must leave for the bank now. Thank you for breakfast."

. . .

She walked quickly from the room and out the door. I wondered if she would return or if this would be the last time I would see her. I thought about her job and my obligations. It was true that there were obstacles to a relationship, but they seemed remote. I could readily imagine having her in my life and holding her in my arms.

I paused to pay the check and strolled out into the street. A half-block away, I saw her stop when she heard the sirens. Three patrol cars blocked her path, and men jumped to the sidewalk, surrounding her and moving her toward one of the cars. Briefly, I saw her shining blond hair disappear inside. The cars sped away, lights flashing. I got into my car, called the airport, and reserved my tickets back to the United States.

El Presidente

"Pedro, do you believe it? We are now in charge of our country. Did you ever believe that the citizens would elect a first-time member of the upper house with only two years' experience as president? Here we are, sitting in the Presidential Palace in the Square Office. The march down Ponce de Leon Boulevard with all of the citizens cheering us was the most exciting thing that has happened to me in my lifetime. We have to do the right thing for our people. It is still surreal that Rafael and Pedro Martinez are going to rule this island country."

"Speaking of ruling the country, we have to make some appointments – fast. My wife and her best friend, Valerie Gillette, want to be my advisors. Miranda wants Valerie to be appointed Secretary, which means everything must go through her before it reaches me. What do you think of that?"

"What is her background?"

"She was in charge of managing apartment buildings in the ghetto for the government, as well as owning some apartments herself. In other words, she was a slum lord."

"That isn't much of a qualification. Let's hope no one checks on her and that they just accept her appointment without comment."

"The next thing I need is someone to be in charge of security. This person will have total control over the armed forces and intelligence agencies and must be someone I can trust completely. That is why you, Pedro, my brother, will take this appointment."

"Okay, Rafael. Consider it done."

"Next, we need someone to be in charge of the Treasury."

"Our cousin Manuel would be a great candidate for this appointment. Let me call him and see if he wants to come back home and be part of our administration."

"We will keep the rest of the employees from the previous administration until we can evaluate them. Since we were able to maintain both the lower and upper house for the FUU Party, I should have no problems getting bills passed. The lower house is headed by a woman whose husband has been given a special tax exemption to bring his products into the country duty free."

"As long as you don't interfere with that arrangement, she will work with you and help you pass the bills that you want."

"The upper house is headed by Enrique Real who has his family working as lobbyists for very large corporations, and they are paid very well for their influence. Also, Enrique bought land at a low price that he knew would be developed and then sold it back to developers at an exorbitant profit. As long as you play ball with him and don't change any of his arrangements, he will also play ball with you. That is basically where we stand right now."

"Let's bring both the leader of the lower house and the upper house in for a meeting as soon as possible."

. . .

"Good morning, Ileana. Good morning, Enrique."

"Good morning, Mr. Presidente."

"I invited you here because I want to get your opinion on a 50-billion-dollar stimulus package to be used for an infrastructure program that I promised the citizens to put them back to work and boost our economy. Since we control both houses, do you think we could get this bill passed?"

"Mr. Presidente, we would have to borrow this money as we are running a deficit now."

"I realize that, but I think we could get the loan from the World Bank."

"Okay, Mr. Presidente, we will get working on it right now. It will certainly boost our economy and will be good for our people."

"One more thing, what would you think about also passing universal healthcare so that all of our people would be covered?"

"It would be very popular, Mr. Presidente and easy to pass, but it might, again, add to our deficit. How much borrowing are you prepared to do? We can't operate running large deficits. Soon, we will be paying more for interest on the debt and will have nothing left over for all our other expenditures."

"I realize that is a problem, but right now, we need to move forward on these two items."

"We understand, Mr. Presidente and will work with you to get these two bills passed."

"Thank you for coming in, and I look forward to working with you in the future. If there is anything I can do to help you, please, just give me a call."

"Thank you, Mr. Presidente."

. . .

"Good morning, Pedro. I have some great news. The World Bank has just approved our application for the 50-billion-dollar loan for the stimulus package. It took two years, but it will be well worth it. Our esteemed Vice-President Miguel Suarez will be organizing it and taking all requests for infrastructure projects and sending them to me for final approval as well as funding. Since the defense budget was reduced, send me projects that you want such as building new living quarters, refurbishing offices, building a non-commissioned officer club, and whatever else you need. Have your personnel suggest them to you and pass them on to me, and I will see to it that the contractors and funding are made available."

"This is going to be great for the morale of both the military and intelligence services, plus it will create more jobs for our people, Mr. Presidente."

"There is one more thing, Pedro, that I would like you to handle for me. As you know better than anyone, my wife is somewhat older than I am, but I married her because her family is not only one of the wealthiest but also one of the most politically powerful in the country. I must admit that I would not be president today if I had not been connected to her family, but I would like to be free of that connection now. Do you understand what I am saying?"

"Yes, I do, Rafael."

"It must be made to look like an accident and must be away from the Presidential Palace. If you need any additional funds, just let me know. I will take them out of the surplus fund."

"I want to bring up a couple of other items with you, Rafael, that I have been hearing, and one is that leaders of both houses are complaining that they cannot reach you whenever something important comes up. They can't get past Valerie Gillette. You'd better come up with a better communication system. Also, I understand that Valerie and the Vice-President have established a very cozy relationship, whatever that means. But, if I were you, I would keep an eye on it."

"Okay, Pedro, thanks for the insight. I am checking Miranda's schedule, and she is giving a speech on Thursday of next week. That may be too soon to arrange everything, but I will try to put things together. I have some ideas of who I can trust to do this. Keep in touch, Pedro, as you are the only one I can actually trust with my life."

. . .

232

"Rafael, this is Pedro. You won't believe what just happened. A car side-swiped Miranda's auto, and it went over a cliff and dropped 100 feet to the bottom. The driver was killed, but Miranda crawled out of the car without a scratch and would not even go to the hospital for a check-up. This is simply amazing. All she keeps saying is that she wants to go back to the palace and talk to you."

"Pedro, I need you to come to the Square Office right away before Miranda gets here. I am going to need your support."

"Okay, I'm on my way."

. . .

"Miranda, it's so good to see you're not injured after such a traumatic experience."

"Rafael, who in the hell is in charge of my security when I am out of the palace?"

"Pedro is responsible for security."

"How the hell could this happen, Pedro? You allowed someone to try to kill me today."

"Don't worry, Miranda, we will find him and charge him with careless driving."

"Careless driving? You two are idiots. This was a murder attempt on me and my driver."

"Have you found the driver of the other car yet?"

"Not yet, but I am certain we will."

"Can you send Valerie in here, please? Valerie, Miranda has been through a traumatic experience today. Will you please take her back to the living quarters and help her to calm down? I will be there as soon as I can. Have someone cancel all my appointments for the rest of the day. Pedro, I want you to issue the following statement to the press corps exactly as I state it: 'The First Lady was involved in an auto accident today, but she was not injured and is safely back at her residence in the Presidential Palace.'"

"Consider it done, Rafael. I am sure you want to be with Miranda now, so I am leaving. Talk to you later."

"Valerie, set up a meeting with the leadership of both houses for tomorrow afternoon. I want to discuss our universal healthcare bill with them."

. . .

"Good afternoon, ladies and gentlemen. It was nice of you to meet with me on such short notice."

"Before we get started, Mr. Presidente, we want to congratulate you on the way you have handled the surplus fund. With all of the infrastructure projects we built and all of the jobs that have been created, our members are extremely happy. It has turned out just as you predicted it would. But, I know we came here to discuss the universal healthcare bill."

"It has been three years, and I just wanted to get an honest assessment of what is transpiring. I am hearing that there is quite a bit of opposition to it, and I want to know exactly what that opposition is and what, if anything, we can do to get this bill moving forward."

"The main opposition from most members of our own FUU Party is that if healthcare is totally free, we will have an influx of illegal aliens from poorer countries coming here for the free healthcare. With our open borders, that is a real possibility and would cost us millions of dollars, which we don't have right now. We are working on a compromise bill which would have all but the poorest citizens and people with preexisting conditions receiving free healthcare. The rest would have to pay and join an exchange that would be set up in each district. We do not have the votes in either house to pass any reform at this time. We will keep working on it and keep you advised. Your setting up a private phone number where we can reach you directly has really been appreciated. We will do all we can, Mr. Presidente."

"Okay, well, thank you again for all of your efforts. Keep me informed as to your progress."

"Rafael, turn on your TV. A helicopter believed to be carrying the first lady has crashed into the ocean. People who witnessed the crash say they heard what sounded like the engine coughing, as though it wasn't getting enough fuel, and then it dropped straight into the ocean. We are awaiting word from the head of security, Pedro Martinez, to confirm our suspicions. Here is the statement now."

"It is with great sorrow that we inform you the First Lady has perished in a helicopter crash. El Presidente is in mourning and will not be available for some time. Tomorrow will be a national day of mourning, and the funeral will be on Friday of this week. That is all we have to say at this time."

"Pedro, I need you to accompany me to the funeral. I have tried to talk to Miranda's family, but they don't seem to want to have anything to do with me. I think they blame me for her demise. Ride with me and stay by my side."

. . .

"I'm glad that is over with. Let's head back to the palace and try to judge what the mood of the people actually is. I hope they don't also blame me for her death."

"I really don't think they do, Rafael. You have always been a great husband to Miranda, and they respect that."

"I hope so, Pedro."

. . .

"Pedro, it has been six months since Miranda's death, so I want you to plant some stories in the press that I am feeling lonely and a little depressed and that you think a presidential ball would be just the thing to cheer me up. Invite single women to attend. Can you do that?"

"Sure, we have many friends in the media. Consider it done."

. . .

"Well, Pedro, I would say the ball was a real success."

"I couldn't help but notice you were dancing with the same girl most of the night."

"Her name is Angelina Atkinson. I really am attracted to her. We plan on having dinner Saturday night, just the two of us. We'll see what happens after that, but I must tell you I'm really excited about seeing her again."

"Don't get too carried away too soon, Rafael."

"Thanks, Pedro. You are always ready with the advice."

. . .

"Rafael, the word has gotten out about you and Angelina. It is being reported that you have a new lady in your life. Since it is no longer a secret, you might as well be seen in public with her if you are really that serious about this relationship."

. . .

"Mr. Presidente, this is Enrique. We have just returned from our three week break and have heard from our representatives their constituents have told them at their town hall meetings that the new healthcare plan has been a total disaster. It was a good thing we put out the details of the bill before we voted on it. When people heard that they were going to have to pay a subscription fee, have high deductibles, would be fined if they did not join the government run exchange and would, in most cases, not be able to use their own doctor, they told our reps that if they voted for this bill, they would be run out of office. Needless to say, there is no way we could ever pass this bill. The people are very happy with our current healthcare system and don't want any changes. The lower house commissioned a poll, and the results were that 70% were against this bill once they were made aware of the specific details."

"Okay, Enrique, I get the message. It was a bad idea on my part. It was one of those things that seems to be a good idea in theory but doesn't work when actually put into practice. We certainly don't want to shove down our citizens' throats something the majority of them do not want just to say we made a major change for our legacy. Can we move on, now, to the defense bill?"

"We definitely need to give our service members and intelligence personnel a wage increase. Also, we need to work on a tax reform bill. We have to lower the corporate tax rate and close most of the loopholes that the special interests have created."

"Okay, Mr. Presidente. We will have both bills on your desk before you leave office."

"Thanks again, Enrique, for all of your hard work. The tax reform bill, along with the shovel ready jobs we are creating, should keep our economy in great shape for the foreseeable future."

. . .

"Pedro, I am going to take Angelina to the presidential beach house on the coast. I would appreciate your sending only a small security detail of two cars, one in front and one behind the limo so as not to attract more attention to our trip than is necessary."

"Are you sure that's what you want, Rafael?"

"I am sure."

"When are you leaving?"

"Two o'clock this afternoon. We will be there for 3 or 4 days."

"Okay, have a good trip."

. . .

"Pedro, this is Captain Morales from the presidential detail. There was an assassination attempt on El Presidente as he was driving to the beach house. A person riding a motorcycle pulled up alongside the limo and started firing at the windows, which were bullet-proof, thank God. We drove our car into the motorcycle killing the rider. He flew up into the air and landed on the highway, killing him instantly. He has no ID, and we think he is someone who came across our open border. The motorcycle was stolen. Unless we can use his fingerprints to ID him, we probably won't know who was responsible for this attack."

"El Presidente is standing here, and he wants to talk to you."

"Pedro, can you meet me back at the Square Office so we can go over what just happened and figure out who might have a reason to try to assassinate me? Angelina is fine, but she wants to go back to her apartment. I told her she would be safer at the palace, but she stated that they were trying to kill me, not her, which I suppose has some logic to it. If you're with me, you might get killed. See you soon."

. . .

"Pedro, who do you think would want to see me dead?"

"It had to be someone who was unaware that our limo is bullet proof. This was a really stupid attempt."

"Maybe it was just to scare me, not really to kill me."

"It could be that someone in Miranda's family still believes you had something to do with her death and took it upon themselves to try to assassinate you. I'm not

238

sure. It could also be your most trusted advisor, Valerie Gillette, who I told you to keep an eye on about a year ago. She is single and thinks you should be paying more attention to her. She also hates the fact that you are dating a white woman. Angelina looks like she was just poured out of a milk carton."

"Pedro, if I thought I would be waking up and finding Valerie Gillette lying next to me each morning, I would arrange for my own assassination. We only have six more months in office, so I think I will just stay in the palace and relax. Vice-President Suarez looks like he is going to be the next president, according to the polls."

. . .

"Pedro, I have been calling Angelina all morning, and she is not answering her cell phone. Can you have someone go by her apartment and check to see if she is alright?"

"Rafael, her apartment is empty, and all her belongings are gone. I checked with British Airways, and they have an Angelina Atkinson listed as having boarded their flight to London this morning. That is the problem with European women. They are very sensitive and, apparently, scare rather easily – although she could see the bullets stuck in the window."

"Well, it was good while it lasted. Thanks, Pedro."

"Manuel, can you come over to the palace tomorrow night for dinner with Pedro and me? I have some things I would like to discuss with you."

"Sure, I'll be there around 6:00."

"Great. See you then."

. . .

"The main reason I wanted you both here is that, as you know, we only have less than six months left, and I wanted to reward both of you for your great loyalty to me

239

during our term in office. I want to know, Manuel, if we could open three secret bank accounts in Switzerland and deposit some funds in them before we leave office."

"That would be a very bad idea, Rafael. There has been a change now in Swiss banking; they can no longer keep account information secret. But, we do have another way of handling this. When I was on Wall Street and we had a client who made a large profit and wanted to shield it from taxes, we recommended that he contact a law firm in the Cayman Islands that would set up a dummy corporation where the actual owner could be anonymous. The client would fly down to the Cayman Islands and open up a bank account using the new corporation. The bank would then give that client a secret pin number made up of letters and numbers that would only be known to the bank and client. No withdrawals from that account could be made without the pin number. I have never heard of a Cayman account being successfully hacked using this method."

"Sounds like a good plan, Manuel. Let's put it into effect as soon as we can."

"I would need you to give me a briefcase with 200,000 in cash - 25,000 for the law firm, 25,000 for the chartered jet to the islands and the rest for deposit for opening the bank accounts. I can make arrangements to do this on a weekend so that no one knows that I have made the trip."

"I will have the briefcase ready for pick up tomorrow afternoon."

"Sounds good. I'll go this weekend."

. . .

"Rafael, I have just gotten back from the islands, and I have Pedro's and your documents with the pin number in an envelope that I will drop off at your office tonight.

We need to discuss exactly how we are going to transfer the money to these accounts."

. . .

"Here are your documents for the accounts in Grand Cayman. What were your ideas on how to transfer the money?"

"I thought we would transfer 150 million from the stimulus fund to the Treasury and have you then transfer 50 million into each of our accounts. Would that work for you?"

"It would have to be done on a Saturday morning. I would use a new laptop computer to make the transfers and then delete the files and take the laptop home with me and make certain it would be totally destroyed, including the hard drive. I would then delete the incoming transfer file so that there would be no record of such a transaction. When the accountants come in Monday morning, the amount of money in the Treasury would be the same as when they left Friday afternoon. No record of any other activity."

"This should work perfectly. We have already burned through 20 billion in the stimulus fund, and much of it was given out in cash payments to contractors to make payroll and buy needed materials, which means our bookkeeping records are such that no one will be able to determine where most of the money was actually disbursed. Let's make our plans for when we will be leaving office and enjoying our private lives."

. . .

"Well, President Suarez, the day has finally arrived for you to take over the reins of the country. I just want to congratulate you. I thought your speech was uplifting for our citizens and am sure you will follow through on all of your promises."

"I am certainly going to try, Rafael. I am keeping Valerie Gillette on as appointment secretary as well as giving her the title of executive administrator of the stimulus fund."

"Where is Valerie now? I want to say goodbye to her."

"She is presently in the living quarters, but I will tell her for you. What are your plans now that you will be a private citizen?"

"Pedro and I are going to charter a plane in a couple of days and fly to London for a three weeks' vacation, which we have not had in five years. He wants to visit colleges that his twins will be attending next year, and I would like to visit the British Isles and just relax."

"What about Manuel?"

"He is flying directly back to New York City and is going back to work on Wall Street, which he loves."

"Well, don't be a stranger. Stop in anytime."

"I know you have many things to do, so I will be going now."

"Best of luck to you."

. . .

"We have just received a new report out of the UK that a plane carrying Pedro and Rafael Martinez is now an hour overdue for its landing time at Heathrow Airport. A full air and sea rescue mission has been launched starting at the point of last contact with the plane. No distress or mayday signals have been received."

. . .

"We have a statement issued by Valerie Gillette on behalf of the Suarez administration that reads as follows: 'The British Navy has called off the sea and air rescue after five days' search. Nothing was found related to this aircraft. Our hearts and prayers go out to Pedro Martinez's wife and children. As for our ex-President, Rafael Martinez, we are certain that he is now reunited with his beloved wife Miranda in heaven."